Amb

Blasts were flying in all directions, pulverizing stone and raising heavy clouds of red Martian dust. It seemed like a hundred of the Aliens were surrounding them, shooting.

Then, just as quickly as it had begun, the shooting stopped. A shadow raced out from behind the Alien ship. Despite its huge head and long arms, it was moving impossibly fast.

The small squadron of Marines could hardly believe their eyes. There was only one Alien—but with a single weapon far more powerful than all of theirs combined. The creature's super-powered gun fired blinding light mortars and left holes in the Martian rock three feet deep.

Without waiting for orders, the Marines opened fire on the thing, but its armor seemed unaffected by the platoon's blasts.

Then the Alien took aim at Shane.

BOOM! Nathan barely saw the blast as the rocket zoomed past him. It clipped Shane's suit, and threw her to the ground. Nathan watched in horror as she squirmed in the red dust. . . .

SPACE: ABOVE AND BEYOND™

#1: The Aliens Approach

a novel by EASTON ROYCE
based on the television series created by
GLEN MORGAN and JAMES WONG
based on the teleplay written by
GLEN MORGAN and JAMES WONG

HarperTrophy
A Division of HarperCollinsPublishers

#1: The Aliens Approach

Prologue

The brilliantly colored rings circling the planet Vesta were far more impressive than the pale rings of Saturn. They swept across the sky at a wild angle, shimmering in the setting sun like a permanent rainbow.

Everything about Vesta was spectacular, from its jagged ice blue moon to its thick jungle brush, greener and denser than any jungle left on Earth.

Millions of people had wanted to be Vesta colonists. Tens of thousands had volunteered. But only two hundred and fifty were chosen for this first mission to settle the stars.

Now, sixteen light-years from Earth, the chosen few stood hand in hand on the planet's surface. Reveling in this strange violet twilight, the colonists prepared to dedicate their colony and claim Vesta in the name of Earth.

Colonial Governor Borman had been a hard task-master back on Earth, drilling each of the would-be colonists in their tasks and procedures. He had made sure that everyone was perfectly trained for this mission—flawlessly ready. But now, as he stood there in the center of the circle, he didn't seem cold and larger than life anymore. He seemed overwhelmed by emotion, just like the rest of them.

As Governor Borman spoke, his voice boomed through the dense, oxygen-rich air. "After a hundred fifty years of calling out, the universe has answered us with tranquil silence, assuring us that humanity alone reaches for the stars." He looked at the collection of joyous faces around him and smiled.

"The silence of the universe is an invitation for us to reach out as far as we dare imagine, and populate every livable star system that we can find."

Around him the colonists tightened their clasped hands, moved by the moment. They were all still wearing their flight coveralls, having not had the time to change since their arrival earlier that day. The rust-colored coveralls displayed the emblem of the Earth over their hearts—an emblem that suddenly seemed more and more important to them as they stood beneath the setting Vestal sun.

"We are a gift to the universe," proclaimed the fledgling colony's governor. "And although the light from our new sun will not reach Earth for sixteen years, we must not grieve for our old lives, but rather rejoice in our future." He turned, catching as many faces as he could.

"There are those back home who say we're here only as a status symbol," he said. "Others call us fortune hunters or say we're running away. But I know we're here because of faith. A faith in each other and in a better world."

Many of the colonists nodded proudly. Yes, this *would* be a better world, a world without the pressures and politics of Earth, a world without poverty. A world where there were still things left to discover. A place of peace.

Two colonists had affixed the flag of Earth to a thin four-foot flagpole. Now they entered the circle and handed the flagpole to Borman.

"The rocket fuel that brought us here can be burned away," continued Borman. "But the belief in ourselves, in one another, and in the future can never be."

Barely able to control his own emotions, Borman held the flagpole high, proclaiming the words that he must have planned from the moment he was chosen for the mission.

"As of today, two suns shine over the human race. Tomorrow may there be a hundred." He brought his hands down and jammed the flagpole into the soft, rich soil.

Thunderous applause rose above the thick Vestal jungle. The joyful noise spread toward the purple-tinged horizon and the shimmering planetary rings beyond.

The sounds of the Vestal night were somewhat like those on Earth, yet at the same time entirely different. There were no crickets, but there was the eerie, eccentric *whirrr* of some insect no one had yet seen. There were no coyotes howling to the ice blue moon that hung heavily in the sky, but some faraway animal did whistle to the night with a strange, singsong melody.

Some colonists were unsettled by the noise, but for the most part they were comforted. The scout ships had found few dangers on the planet. No large predators, and no bacteria that human antibodies couldn't handle. With nothing to fear in paradise, most of the colonists had little problem falling asleep. After all, it had been an exhausting day for them.

They had unloaded cargo from most of the ship and had erected the small prefab huts that they would live in until they had a chance to build more permanent structures. The high level of oxygen in the atmosphere had kept them giddy and wakeful for a while, but their own tired bodies couldn't fight off sleep.

No one in hut number five was awake when the clock struck fifteen—the new hour for two A.M. on this strange and wonderful world. Had any of the colonists been awake, they might have seen the dark figure standing silhouetted against the cold moonlight in the doorway. They might have seen it slowly making its way down the narrow aisle between their cots, its breath so hot it steamed in the thick Vestal air. The dark, powerful form studied the sleeping humans before stalking out and disappearing in the rustling leaves of the forest.

Five minutes later, three dots appeared in the sky. Three tiny slits of light, moving in formation, growing larger in size as they approached the unsuspecting Vesta colony. . . .

But even before the engines of those spacecraft could be heard, ground forces were in place. The sound of approaching footsteps startled some of the colonists in hut number five, and they awoke. *It must be one of the night guards*, they assumed drowsily. *They're checking to make sure everything's secure.*

They had no way of knowing that the colonists chosen for the first night's watch were already dead.

The footsteps stopped for a brief instant.

BOOM! An explosion shook the corrugated steel frame of the hut, awakening everyone in the colony. The steel door of the hut blew off its hinges and slammed to the ground. A creature, tall and angular, covered in black armor, stood in the doorway.

The colonists barely had a chance to scream before the Alien raised its weapon and shot a stream of fire that burned through everyone and everything in its path. Suddenly the strange, unearthly sounds of the Vestal night were replaced by the all-too-earthly sound of human screams and wails of agony. The invaders blasted their way into all fifteen huts, setting them aflame in less than a Vestal minute. Bursting from the burning huts, the colonists fled in all directions. But they were running from an enemy they knew nothing about and could barely see in the dark—and they had nowhere to run. If sixteen light-years had seemed like a long way from Earth before, it felt like a whole universe away now.

Up above the carnage, the three warplanes were still flying in formation. Engines screaming, they smashed through the thin blue cloud cover, coming in low over the colony for a strafing run.

They blasted anything and everything that moved with pinpoint accuracy. The warplanes were like nothing anyone had ever seen. The black tri-winged ships flew faster than any man-made fighter and seemed almost like living beasts breathing fire. It took them only two passes to set the entire colony aflame.

A handful of colonists ran to the radio to transmit a call for help. Before they could even begin, one of the Alien troopers aimed his weapon at the communications device and reduced it to a useless, melted lump.

As the horrified survivors watched, the huge satellite dish that was their last connection to Earth became the next target of the three fighter ships above. Spinning through the swirling smoke and flames, each ship fired a single blast. The dish went up in a ball of flame, leaving only tiny chunks of singed metal where it had stood.

But the intruders were not done yet. Next, they

took aim at the great colony transport ship. The mighty hull of the *Giant Star* vessel had survived the violent, wrenching forces of the trans-Vestal wormhole on its trip from Earth. But after three combined blasts from the screeching warplanes, the once-grand vessel disintegrated into a smoldering heap.

In the center of what was once the Vesta colony, Governor Borman screamed frantic orders, trying to group the few remaining colonists into battle against this unknown enemy. But it was too late. With a panther-like precision, one of the Alien shock troopers mercilessly turned its weapon on the governor, cutting him down. Then, without a second thought, the creature took aim at the flapping flag of Earth—the flag that Borman had proudly raised just a few short hours before. With one blast, the flag burned brightly in the oxygen-rich atmosphere of Vesta. Its tattered embers drifted into a night sky filled with the harsh, unfeeling light of the ice moon.

Chapter 1

Ninety-six trillion miles from the doomed Vesta colony, on a blue planet called Earth, three humans were preparing to change the course of the human race—only they didn't know it yet. . . .

The first hid, knees to chest, cramped in a storage crate aboard a forty-six-story interstellar craft, counting down the final seconds to launch. His name was Nathan West, and the plastic crate he sat in had, until a short time earlier, contained hydroponic supplies.

As far as Nathan, or anyone else on Earth knew, the Vesta mission had been an unparalleled success. Communication had been temporarily lost, but that was just a small glitch.

Now, the second interstellar colony was to be set up in the Tellus system. The new planet boasted eight moons and a waterfall six times as wide as Niagara—or so the early scouts had reported.

All systems were go aboard the Tellus interstellar transport. The entire world was watching the proceedings with breathless anticipation. Watching, especially, the two hundred and fifty colonists—just like the Vesta mission—on board, strapped into their padded seats, knuckles white as they listened to the final countdown.

Except there weren't two hundred and fifty colonists on the ship. Nathan West was the two hundred and fifty-*first* person on board. And that was his problem—the biggest problem he had had to face since signing up for the colonization project.

It's amazing how quickly a man can go from being a national hero to desperate stowaway. For Nathan, it happened faster than a ship could pass through a wormhole.

Nathan had been the jewel of the colonial program. Smart, well-liked, a quick learner, he was just the sort of young recruit the colonies were looking for.

He had originally been assigned to the Vesta colony, but he'd turned it down so that he could be with his girlfriend, Kylen, on the Tellus trip.

Nathan had been in love with Kylen Celina for as long as he could remember. They were a rare and perfect pair in a world where few things seemed to last anymore. They had applied for the colonization program on a whim—and when they both made the list it proved something to them—something that they had suspected for a long time: they were destined to be together forever.

But that was a long time ago. Those memories

were marred by a more recent incident. Nathan could still hear the awful words that Overmeyer, the soon-to-be governor of Tellus, had spoken just the day before:

"You and Kylen fought for the rights of the In-Vitros," Overmeyer had said, his voice filled with accusation. "And now, thanks to you, we're being forced to take ten of them to Tellus. We'll have to leave ten of our original crew behind."

But that wasn't the worst of it. One of them—either Nathan or Kylen—would have to stay behind. Only one of them could make the trip.

They had sworn they would live their lives together, and now they would be separated by hundreds of trillions of miles.

No! No matter what Overmeyer said, whatever the risk, Nathan could never allow that to happen. And so, they had devised a plan. While Kylen took her place among the colonists at T-minus one hour, Nathan found his way into the cargo bay. He could only pray that the tightly packed, pressurized hold would have enough oxygen to last him for the trip to Tellus.

He had no other choice. His life wouldn't be worth living without Kylen. He knew that. Overmeyer had offered him a position in the Marine Corps Space Cavalry, and there was a slight chance that the Marines would eventually join the colonists. But Nathan needed more than a slight chance. He needed to be on this ship with Kylen, no matter what it took. No matter how many rules he had to break.

Little did he know as he sat there, crammed into his hiding place, that the countdown had stopped. When the ship's computers had detected almost two hundred pounds of extra weight, the launch was halted. Before Nathan suspected that anything was wrong, security forces were already running down the gantry catwalk with life-sign sensors, heading right for Nathan's hiding place.

He heard them climb down into the hold, but it was too late to escape. They ripped open the face of his small storage box and jerked him out of the cargo hold. It didn't matter how well-liked he had been before. Now he was a stowaway. A criminal. They treated him with cruel disdain.

As they hauled him past the colonists—those lucky two hundred and fifty, still strapped in their chairs—Nathan caught sight of Kylen. When she saw him, she wrestled herself out of her safety harness and tried to run to him. But she was held back by security guards.

"Nathan!" she cried. She reached for him, but the security officers hustled Nathan past before she could get close.

He pulled an arm free from the heavy hands holding him, reached into his pocket, and pulled out a piece of paper. It was a letter folded small enough to fit in his palm. He tossed it to Kylen.

"I'll find you," Nathan screamed, struggling against the guards. "I *will* find you!"

The sight of Kylen's tears were almost too much for him to stand, but he could not look away from her. She reached around her neck and yanked off the phototag she wore there. Nathan dug in his heels against the airlock threshold.

"Nathan!" she cried again. "I believe in you." She threw him the tag as they pulled him out of the ship.

The heavy hatch came down between them, sealing the great ship closed with Kylen inside. For the first time, Nathan realized how desperately different his life would now be.

They drove him to the perimeter gate of the launch complex and cast him out with nothing more than the pack he had arrived with on his first day. They left him there, alone, without so much as an apology for having destroyed his life so completely.

As he stood there, Nathan felt something strange under his feet—a vibration that tore at his soul. Around him trees rattled, sending flocks of birds heading in terror for the skies.

The launch. He could see it taking off in the distance, a plume of white smoke arcing across the sky. He watched until it disappeared into the heavens, taking Kylen as far away as two people have ever been. . . .

Yet even now, in his moment of defeat, another

plan was emerging. They had offered him flight training with the Space Cavalry—and it was rumored that the cavalry might be sent for sentry missions to the colonies before the wormholes closed. It hadn't sounded like an option a few hours ago. But if that was the only way to get out there, then it was the path he had to choose.

"I will be with you, Kylen," he whispered to himself. "Even if I have to tear a new hole in space myself. I'll find you."

Chapter 2

Far away, in the City of Brotherly Love, Cooper Hawkes raced through a dark construction site, the object of old-fashioned hate. He was the second one born to save the world, although many would say he wasn't born at all, but rather hatched—from a tempered glass gestation tank.

Cooper was an In-Vitro, a being created without the luxury of parents for the sole purpose of fighting in the Artificial Intelligence War. But, as everyone knows, the In-Vitro project was an unparalleled failure. The In-Vitros, who were bred for war, refused to fight. And when the AI Wars were finally won without their help twenty years ago, the In-Vitros became an underclass in every society, despised by the very people who brought them into the world.

So it was no wonder that Cooper Hawkes spent much of his time running for his life.

He had been hired on the construction crew of the hundred-and-forty-five-story Philadelphia Center just a few days before. He figured he might get a few weeks of work in before the crew suspected he was an In-Vitro and hurled him out into the gutter. No such luck. He had been there only three days before they found him out.

He could hear the footsteps behind him as he ran. He was fast, but there were too many of them, coming from too many different directions. He leaped past the billboard showing the spectacular tower he had almost had a hand in creating. His shadow slid across the brightly lit billboard and back into the dark night.

BANG! He landed hard on the tower's foundation—but the pain of the fall didn't stop him. He had always been tough. He used the pain to push himself forward, away from the bloodthirsty men chasing him.

As he raced out of the construction site and into a dark alley, he slammed into a homeless man and his shopping cart, sending the cart flying.

"What the . . ." the old man hollered. But Cooper had no time for an apology. And if he had, he wouldn't have apologized anyway. Remorse and compassion were not a part of his emotional vocabulary.

His pursuers were closing in. Cooper crashed through a steel door—but he only found himself back in the construction site, where the polymeric graphite girders of the skeletal tower rose toward the moonless sky.

The moment he crashed through the door he realized his mistake. He hadn't worked there long enough to know the terrain, the best paths of flight. But his pursuers had all been there for weeks. They knew every inch of the site. It would be only a matter of time before they found him.

A foot came flying out of nowhere, catching Cooper in his gut and bringing him down. He retaliated with a kick to the kneecap. His assailant yelped with pain and buckled to the ground. Cooper scrambled to his feet and took off—but he'd been slowed down just enough for the others to catch up with him. Before he could go two steps they were on either side of him. They grabbed him and threw him hard to the ground. His face, already bruised, grew a new welt as it hit the hard plasti-crete floor.

Two men wrenched his hands behind his back as he lay on the ground, pulling his arms nearly out of their sockets.

Behind him, he heard Davis, the leader of the deadly little squad, say two words that chilled Cooper down to his aching bones.

"Check him!"

A knee jabbed into his spine. Cooper struggled hard, but he couldn't stop them from grabbing the back of his long hair and pulling it up. There was a circular naval at the base of his skull. It was the one telltale sign that he was an In-Vitro.

While the others held him, Davis stalked close. "I knew it," said Davis. "A *Tank*. I can smell 'em—like an animal."

Davis's voice was deep and rang with the kind of hatred that cried of murder. "I told the foreman not to hire him," he growled. "Get him up!"

The two others pulled Cooper to his feet so Davis could look him in the face.

"I had two uncles die in the AI Wars 'cause the Tanks wouldn't fight," snarled Davis.

"I was still in the tank," insisted Cooper, who hadn't really been "born" until he'd been pulled from the tank when he was eighteen. "I had nothin' to do with the war!"

Davis tossed him a crooked grin. "Then you're even more worthless than I thought."

"I never asked to be born," Cooper reminded him.

"Too bad," said Davis. "But now you can ask to die."

The others looped a steel chain around Cooper's neck.

"Go on," said Davis. "Ask."

Even in the dim light, Cooper could almost see himself reflected in Davis's eyes. A pathetic waste of life. That's how everyone saw him. He had lived a useless existence; he would die a meaningless death. And no one would mourn his death, any more than people would mourn when the tanks that gave birth to the In-Vitros were sold for scrap metal.

No mother, no father, no soul.

That's what people said about the In-Vitros. Cooper

didn't know whom he hated more—himself, or these men who were trying to kill him.

He spat in Davis's face.

The thugs tossed the thick chain over a girder and yanked Cooper up by his neck. He was starting to feel the effects of his oxygen being cut off when, four feet above the ground, he realized that his feet were in perfect position to deliver some serious damage.

Whether Cooper Hawkes had a soul or not, he wasn't going to die this way.

He kicked out, catching one of the men in the jaw, and the other in the nose. They both flew backward, letting go of the chain.

Cooper fell to the ground with a thud. He ripped his hands free of the fiber-optic wire they had used to bind him and wrenched the chain from his neck. Now there was only Davis.

Before Cooper could even get his bearings, Davis swung a metal pole at him, just missing his head. But on his next swing, Cooper was ready. He caught the pole in mid-swing and pulled it from Davis's hands.

Davis turned and ran.

Cooper was right behind him as he dashed out of the construction site and back into the street. Now it was *Davis's* turn to ask to die. Cooper held the pole out, ready to swing at anything that came out of the shadows.

A loud screech pierced the night as an armored

police car came flying down the alley, sirens full blast. The police were supposed to protect In-Vitros the same way they protected and served other citizens. But Cooper knew that they wouldn't be on his side.

The car screamed to a halt in front of the two men. Davis quickly pulled open the back door and jumped in, begging the police for protection. Cooper was filled with a rage so intense he lost control. He brought the heavy pipe down on the hood of the armored car. Unable to stop himself, he swung the pipe again.

SMASH! He shattered the side window that Davis was peering through.

"Get out of there!" Cooper screamed, wanting to make Davis's head the next target of the pipe. It wasn't just Davis he wanted to pulverize. It was all of them— every last human being who had spit at him, who had looked at him as if he were an animal.

A policeman leaped from the car and aimed a heavy black weapon at Cooper. Davis saw his chance to escape. He jumped out of the car and disappeared down the dark alley.

"He tried to hang me!" Cooper screamed, still waving the metal club. The officer responded with cold, unfeeling eyes. Davis must have told them that he was a Tank. They would never believe his side of the story now.

Unable to control his anger, Cooper smashed down on the car again, this time shattering the windshield.

POP! He heard a gun fire. He didn't realize he'd been shot until he felt the shock-dart puncture deep into his chest. As he slipped out of consciousness, he suddenly realized that he should have let Davis kill him. Because nowadays they were sentencing the bad-seed In-Vitros to a punishment worse than any prison.

They were going to send him into the military.

Chapter 3

It never stopped raining in Southern California. Perhaps that was why no one wanted to live there anymore. San Diego was no exception to the rule.

In the dead of the stormy night, a young woman climbed through a hole in the rusty fence that surrounded the crumbling ruins of a house.

Her name was Shane Vansen, and she was twenty-one. She was the third who would shape humanity's future, and although her destiny lay among the stars, it wasn't her future she was considering just then. It was her past.

The ruined door swung open to reveal the shell of a house that leaked like a sieve. Sixteen years of termites and endless rains had taken their toll. It was hard for her to believe she had spent the first six years of her life here.

Holding a bouquet of wet flowers, she walked toward the master bedroom—her parents' room. She could still imagine her father standing there, tall and handsome in his Marine sergeant's uniform. She could remember his face on that last night: stern eyes camouflaging his terror as the enemy AI troops closed in.

They had turned off the lights, and her mother had spirited Shane and her two younger sisters up into the attic.

"Take care of them," her mother told Shane, and then whispered, "I love you," before she shut them up in the attic and went down to be with Shane's father.

From the attic, Shane had heard the door being kicked in. She had watched with her sisters through the grill as the AI commander droned to her parents, *"Kneel!"* In that chilling electronic voice that sounded like fingernails scratching out words on a blackboard.

She had had to bite her lip to keep from screaming as she watched the AI troops raise their guns to her mother's and father's heads. She'd had to hold her hand over her sister's mouth to keep her quiet as well. Her sister had bitten deep into her hand as those guns went off. Her parents had been executed with the cold precision that the AIs were well-known for.

Now, sixteen years later, all that was left of the house was this crumbling ruin that would soon be washed away by the rains. Yet the memories were still fresh and just as painful.

Shane left the bundle of flowers on the spot where her parents were murdered. She'd wanted to believe they died for something but still couldn't figure out what that might be. It was a question that had plagued Shane ever since they died.

She had done what her mother had asked. She had taken care of her sisters, whether they wanted to be taken care of or not. Now it was time for her to do something for herself. So she had enlisted in the Marines, like her father before her, and joined the Space Cavalry. Maybe there she would find purpose. Maybe there, controlling the turbulent engines of a fighter jet, she might find some level of peace in her soul.

She heard a jet pass by above, its low rumble like distant thunder, both threatening and comforting at the same time. There was a hole in the roof, and through that hole she could see stars. As she peered at those stars through the breaking storm clouds, she began to sense something beginning to unfold in her life—not just a new beginning, but a new destiny she could not yet see.

Shane wondered if her life would make any difference in the vast, unknowable universe. She wondered whether or not one's destiny was something you were born into, or something you create. Perhaps the Space Cavalry would give her the answer.

Chapter 4

"I AM SERGEANT MAJOR BOUGUS. I AM YOUR SENIOR DRILL INSTRUCTOR. I AM HERE TO TURN YOU SLIMY CIVILIAN CESSPOOL PARASITES INTO UNITED STATES MARINE CORPS SPACE AVIATORS, INVOKING BOWEL-WRENCHING TERROR INTO THE DARK HEARTS OF YOUR ENEMIES."

Bougus had begun screaming in fine military fashion from the moment they stepped out of the bus on the tarmac of the Loxley, Alabama, Marine base. Actually, they didn't "step" out of the bus, but rather they were flushed out by two human pit bulls in Marine uniforms. Now they all stood at attention, a mismatched crew of Marine wannabees.

"WHY ARE YOU HERE?" shouted Bougus into the face of an African-American girl name Vanessa Damphousse.

"Uh, sir, to find a direction, sir!" she said, with far less force in her voice than Bougus liked.

"A DIRECTION?" Bougus demanded. "ARE YOU LOST?"

Damphousse's shoulders sagged slightly out of the tight attention she had been holding.

"Sir, I, uh . . . suffer from a sense of disconnection, and—"

"ANSWER THE QUESTION!" Everyone stiffened back to attention as he shouted.

Damphousse didn't dare look him in the face again. "Sir, yes I am, sir! Lost, sir!"

"DO I LOOK LIKE A ROAD MAP TO YOU?"

"Sir, no, sir!"

"WELL, I AM A ROAD MAP!" proclaimed Bougus.

Further down the line, Shane Vansen and Nathan West watched, relieved that he had not chosen to single them out . . . yet.

A number of them had met on the long bus ride out. Nathan and Shane had hit it off right away. Perhaps there was something similar about that world-weary look in their eyes that drew them to one another.

Bougus stalked back down the line, looking over each and every recruit. "I AM YOUR PERSONAL ROAD MAP," he bellowed. "I WILL LEAD AND YOU WILL FOLLOW! I WILL TEACH AND YOU WILL LEARN! WHEN YOU LEAVE MY ACADEMY, YOU WILL BE WEAPONS—FOCUSED AND FULL OF PURPOSE! HOT-ROD ROCKET JOCKS OF PRECISION AND STRENGTH TEARING ACROSS THE COSMOS!"

Far behind Bougus, the recruits caught sight of a single Squadron crossing the tarmac. Dressed in black with black berets, they had an elite air about them, as if they didn't walk on the same ground as everyone else. It didn't take a genius to know who they were—the 127th Attack Wing, the "Angry Angels." Even among civilians, the 127th was legend. Every schoolkid had seen the video of them storming the AI strongholds all those years ago, almost single-handedly turning the war. Of course, all the faces had changed since then, but the reputation of the 127th remained the same. They were the best there ever were, or ever would be.

"That's why I joined," Shane whispered to Nathan as the Angry Angels strode out of view. "Someday," she added, "that will be me."

"Yeah," said the wide-eyed recruit standing next to them. His name was Mike Pagodin, but everyone called him "Pags." Kind of like a dog. The nickname made sense: he seemed way too enthusiastic about everything and was always eager to please—just like a friendly pup.

"Hey," Pags whispered to Nathan with a goofy smile on his face. "When do you think we'll get our planes?"

At the far end of the line, Bougus was tormenting Paul Wang, the most intimidated of the group.

"LET ME HEAR YOUR WAR CRY!" shouted Bougus.

Wang had to give him three terrified yelps before Bougus invited the two drill instructors over to scream in Wang's ears, letting him experience the joy of real Marine war cry in stereo. Then Bougus marched back down the line toward Shane and Nathan.

"IN SPACE," announced Bougus, "NO ONE CAN HEAR YOU SCREAM—UNLESS IT'S THE WAR CRY OF A UNITED STATES MARINE!"

His eyes caught Shane's. She stiffened, determined to stand toe-to-toe with the sergeant and not be made a fool of.

"WHY DID YOU JOIN MY CORPS?" Bougus demanded. A fine spray of spittle accompanied his words.

"Sir, to defend my country, sir!" replied Shane, thinking it must be the only perfect answer.

"TO DEFEND YOUR COUNTRY?" mocked Bougus. "ARE YOU CRAZY? WE HAVE NO ENEMIES! YOU'VE MADE A TERRIBLE MISTAKE!"

Shane refused to be intimidated. "Sir, the best way to maintain peace is to maintain a strong defense! Sir!"

Bougus showed no sign of being impressed. "ARE YOU RUNNING FOR OFFICE, PRIVATE?"

Beside Shane, Nathan snickered. He couldn't help it. He was amazed that Bougus could keep a straight face himself when he did this.

Bougus's eyes snapped to Nathan. "DO I AMUSE YOU?"

"Sir, no sir!" shouted Nathan.

"THEN AMUSE *ME*!" demanded Bougus. "TWENTY-FIVE PUSH-UPS—NOW!"

Which, of course, made Shane snicker. In an instant, Bougus had her doing push-ups right beside Nathan.

Cooper Hawkes watched this exercise as his Jeep approached the group. He knew all the recruits could see the cuffs on his wrists before the MPs removed them.

When Bougus saw him, he strode over and spoke softly, so only Cooper could hear. Which, in its own way, was far worse than being screamed at.

"I know all about you, Hawkes," said Bougus. Although he whispered, somehow his voice had the same intensity as when he shouted. "So now the judges think it's funny to sentence Tanks to the Marines."

Cooper slouched, refusing to stand at attention, refusing to look at him. With the bruise from the shock-dart still aching in his chest, he was in no mood to deal with a war-grizzled drill sergeant.

"I want you to know," continued Bougus, "that I fought alongside the Tanks in the AI War, and I know they're lazy and don't care about anyone, or anything."

Cooper grinned out of the corner of his mouth. "Well then, I won't let you down."

Bougus didn't take too kindly to the words or to the grin. He turned so everyone could hear and

28

shouted, "THE ONLY THING YOU'RE GONNA LET DOWN IS YOUR FACE, ON THE DECK! GIMME FIFTY!"

The two drill instructors pushed Cooper to the ground, right beside Nathan and Shane. Cooper turned and caught Shane looking at him, so he winked at her. As he expected, she looked away, disgusted.

Good, thought Cooper. *Maybe this isn't going to be a total waste.*

At the sight of Cooper beside him, Nathan picked up the pace. He had no love of Tanks now that the Tanks were responsible for tearing him and Kylen apart.

"ONE, TWO, THREE, FOUR, I LOVE THE MARINE CORPS!" chanted Bougus, trying to keep them in rhythm.

Cooper, Nathan, and Shane rose and fell in unison—the first three chosen for punishment. Perhaps it was a little more than coincidence. Not even Sergeant Major Bougus could know how important the three Marines he had dropped to the deck would be.

Chapter 5

In the coldness of space, where the sun is one-tenth its size from Earth, and the Earth itself is just a blue pinprick among star-filled heavens, the Tellus probe slingshot around Neptune toward the trans-Tellus wormhole. They were four weeks into the mission: right on schedule.

The two hundred and fifty colonists buckled themselves in and prepared for trans-Tellus injection. It would be more jarring than blast-off, they were told, more jarring than anything they had ever experienced—except, perhaps, for birth itself.

The ship rattled and groaned as it entered the wormhole, buffeted by the violent waves of folded space. The colonists could feel their flesh twisting, stretching, and folding. Finally the ship burst out into a place so far from Earth it would take a hundred lifetimes just to count the miles.

Before them, one of Tellus's many crater-filled moons eclipsed the planet. But soon their ship came around the moon, and they saw a glorious world of green and gold—their new home.

Thrusters came on full force as the ship rocketed toward the planet.

"Prepare for entry." The captain's announcement was met with cheers from the colonists.

Excitement and anticipation filled the immense cabin like an electric surge. The colonists were ready for anything now.

Almost anything.

Tightly strapped into her chair, Kylen Celina pulled out a crumpled piece of paper from her flight-suit pocket. It was Nathan's letter, the one he had given to her as he was pulled away from the ship.

It wasn't like Nathan to write love letters. Still, she would cherish it, for it was all she had left of him.

They say in five billion years, the sun will burn most of its hydrogen, the letter began, *and in another few million years, the sun will expand, swallowing Mercury, and Venus, and finally the Earth, until at last the sun collapses in upon itself, becoming a red dwarf and growing dimmer and dimmer. Elsewhere, new stars are born, older systems thrive, and our sun dies. If that's how long it takes—*

BOOM! There was a flash of light, followed by a blast of heat. Then nothing but screams.

Kylen turned. A whole section of the multi-leveled cabin collapsed. Dozens of her fellow colonists were crushed in their chairs, pinned beneath heavy layers of graphite and steel.

"What's happening?!" she screamed.

BOOM! A second blast rocked the ship.

Flames suddenly sprang up from beneath her chair, burning her through the fabric. Frantically she tore at her harness to get free.

She leaped from the chair just as it was engulfed in flames. Around her, others were scrambling for fire extinguishers to save those still trapped.

Still clutching the letter from Nathan, Kylen crawled across the floor away from the fire. Another blast hit far above them. *We're being attacked*, she thought. *But by whom? It can't be possible.*

She reached out and grasped a broken, twisted pole sticking from the floor and held on, waiting for death, hoping it would be quick and painless.

There were no windows to show them the Squadron outside. A dozen triple-winged fighters had descended from the heavens and attacked the defense-less Tellus transport. There was no doubt what their intentions were.

The captain and navigator were the only two on board who had seen the ominous Alien crafts before the blast hit the bridge and blew it apart.

The Squadron of Alien fighters circled again. With the bridge demolished, they now took aim at the engines. The powerful explosion as the fuel cells blew sent the ship careening toward the Tellurian atmosphere at a dangerously steep angle.

Merciless in their attack, the fighters came around again and again, blowing massive holes in the cargo bay, the hydroponic unit, and finally the cabin. Doomed colonists were sucked out into space through the gaping hole. The dying ship spun end over end, growing red hot as it fell through the atmosphere of the green planet.

In another part of the galaxy, a glassy, black, star-speckled sky was shredded by a Squadron of Marine Corps starjets. Six attack fighters screamed across space in tight formation, sharp and sleek. Their thrusters perfectly mimicked aerodynamics, making them far more maneuverable in the vacuum of space than any ship had been before.

Nathan sat in his cockpit viewing the starfield before him. Even though most of the ship's functions were keyed to the movement of his eyes and sublingual voice commands, there were still a thousand buttons and readouts for him to consider.

Unidentified ships suddenly descended from the stars above him.

"This is Red Leader," announced Nathan. "Bandits at two o'clock confirmed."

"Red Leader, this is Red-three," announced Shane from her cockpit. She was perhaps the most comfortable of all of them in her current surroundings. "I confirm. AOA fifteen degrees."

"R-four confirm," announced Pags, who sat in his cockpit like a kid finally let into a candy store. "Check six. I can't find him."

Five fighters took an intercept course toward the enemy, but as Nathan checked his screen, he realized Pags was right: Red-six was nowhere to be seen.

"R-five, check six!" ordered Nathan. "Where's Hawkes?"

"R-five confirm," responded Damphousse. "No sign of him."

Nathan tried to get his screen to show a wider area of space, but he couldn't waste time with that now—not with the enemy assuming attack position right in front of him.

"Wang! Is he behind you?"

"Negative, Red Leader!"

Nathan saw the starfield spinning before him. Although slightly nauseated by the pitch of the roll, all he could feel was his anger toward Cooper flaring. "*Hawkes!*"

At a safe distance from the battle, flying a parallel course, Cooper Hawkes watched with amusement as his comrades tried to engage the enemy. With one hand on the controls, he leaned back and comfortably rested on his elbow. He shifted the controls back and forth, enjoying the rocking motion, and enjoying the fact that everybody was wondering what in the world he was doing.

"Enemy craft have locked on to us!" he heard Shane say.

Cooper watched as his comrades rolled out of the enemy gunsights, just in time.

"Hawkes, dammit! Where are you?" he heard Nathan shout over the radio.

At last Cooper decided he might as well give them what they wanted. He pulled back on his stick and headed toward the Squadron—*directly* toward the Squadron, firing his thrusters and picking up speed.

The enemy zoomed around him. In front of him he could see his own Squadron trying to regroup.

"There he is," said Shane.

"What is he doing?" Pags yelled.

Cooper gave the ship more power.

Before Nathan could take any evasive action, Hawkes cut across his starboard side, tearing off his wing.

"NO!" screamed Nathan as his engine detonated. The two ships went up in fireballs.

Shane and Pags tried to fly clear, but fragments of debris hit them both and their ships went up too. Damphousse and Wang collided. The six fireballs merged, becoming a single grand fireball in the black starlit sky.

The canopy of Cooper's starjet cockpit opened to reveal Sergeant Major Bougus standing where the wing should have been.

"YOU'RE DEAD!" Bougus screamed in Cooper's face—not with mock military anger but with real anger. "YOU'RE DEAD! THE ENTIRE SQUADRON IS DEAD—BECAUSE OF YOU!"

Cooper leaned back. He couldn't care less. Around them, the canopies of the other simulators opened.

"You stupid Tank," Nathan shouted the second his canopy was up.

Bougus turned to Nathan, fire in his eyes. "YOU SHUT UP! YOU'RE DEAD!"

Cooper hopped out of his simulator and crossed his arms. "Who cares? It ain't real."

"SOMEDAY," yelled Bougus, "IT WILL BE REAL! YOU'LL BE IN THE MIDDLE OF A HAIRY FUR BALL, *AND YOU WILL DIE*! WITH YOU AROUND, THE SQUAD DOESN'T HAVE TO FEAR THE ENEMY, JUST YOU! *JUST YOU*!"

By now everyone had climbed out of their simulators.

"I should have blown you away," grumbled Nathan.

To Nathan's surprise, Bougus turned on him. "IS THAT RIGHT? GET OVER HERE!" Then Bougus turned to the rest of them. "EVERYONE! OVER HERE NOW!"

They all lined up before their simulator cockpits. Cooper of course was the last, pushing his way between Shane and Nathan.

Bougus looked Nathan in the eye. Nathan stood at attention but didn't try to hide his anger.

"GRAB HAWKES'S BUTT!" ordered Bougus.

Nathan wasn't quite ready for that command. He hesitated.

"THAT'S AN ORDER!" screamed Bougus, hitting his stride. "GRAB IT! EVERYONE GRAB THE BUTT OF THE GUY TO YOUR RIGHT."

Reluctantly everyone reached out their right hand and did as they were ordered.

"YOU FEEL THAT?" demanded Bougus. "THAT'S YOUR OWN BUTT IN YOUR HAND! HIS IS YOURS, AND HERS IS YOURS, AND YOURS IS HIS," he said, pointing at everyone right down the line.

"YOU MAY FLY IN INDIVIDUAL ROCKETS, BUT YOU'RE A SQUADRON, A TEAM!" roared Bougus, pacing back and forth along the line. "IF YOU RISK YOUR BUTT, YOU RISK THE TEAM'S. YOU PEOPLE HAVE BEEN HERE SIX WEEKS, AND STILL YOU DO NOT KNOW HOW TO WORK TO-GETHER. AND IF YOU DON'T LEARN, THAT FATTY CLUMP OF FLESH IN YOUR HAND WILL BE BLOWN TO EVERY SPECK OF THE GALAXY, AND YOUR OWN WILL BE RIGHT BEHIND!"

Then Pags, who could find the bright side of a black hole, spoke up, "Sir, maybe Cooper would do better in a real plane, sir."

Cooper grinned at that. He didn't expect anyone to stand up for him.

"YOU'VE GOT TO BE KIDDING ME!" screamed Bougus. "I'M AFRAID OF YOU IN A *SIMULATOR*.

NOW GET BACK IN YOUR PITS! WE'LL DO IT AGAIN UNTIL WE DO IT RIGHT! MOVE!"

Nathan released his hold on Cooper's behind, and they eyed each other with all the contempt they could muster. As far as Nathan was concerned, his hatred of Cooper was well-earned. And from where Cooper stood, he had more than enough reason to hate Nathan West, who was clean-cut, respected, and everything Cooper Hawkes could never be.

Hating each other was easy. The hard part would be learning to trust each other enough to fly into battle.

Chapter 6

The Asteroid Belt sat on a lonely strip of rural road between Loxley, Alabama, and the Marine base. So of course the diner catered to Marines. It was one of the few places where flyers and recruits could loosen up and let down from their high tension lives, and so it was always packed.

Nathan, Shane, and the other recruits had finally succeeded in their simulation that day, in spite of Cooper's disinterest and his sluggish control of his craft. The fact that they got through it at all was reason to celebrate, so they went out that night to Asteroid's.

Cooper, of course, was not included, but he showed up anyway. He sauntered past the table where Nathan and Shane sat and took a seat at the counter.

"He's like a shark," Damphousse suggested. "I think he likes being alone."

Shane shook her head. "No one *really* likes being alone."

Nathan glanced over at Cooper. "Yeah, well some things are better left that way."

Shane shrugged. She wanted to feel sorry for

Cooper, but he was so unpleasant about everything that she found it hard feeling anything for him but anger. But then maybe that's what he wanted people to feel. Maybe his nastiness was a smoke screen to keep people from feeling anything else. Because, after all, dealing with hatred was what Cooper did best. It was easy for him. He'd probably have no idea how to deal with somebody actually liking him. If someone ever did.

The door of the bar opened. In strutted six figures dressed entirely in black. If it's possible to sit at attention, that's what Shane did.

Meanwhile, Pags began talking about planes again. "If I ran the military," he said, "I'd give us our planes the first day."

Shane nudged him to be quiet. "The Angry Angels." She nodded toward the six figures.

The Angels approached a crowded table. Without saying a word, the Marines sitting there got up and let the Angels sit down.

Shane was completely awestruck as she watched them, but Nathan was less impressed. No matter how good he got, Nathan hoped he would never be that full of himself.

Even Cooper, who was far more observant than he let on, noticed them as they entered. He also noticed that one of them, McQueen, came to the counter and sat alone.

McQueen was different from the other Angels.

He was a quiet loner, a bit mysterious. Like Cooper.

Cooper tried to imagine himself in a year's time, part of a tightly knit fighting Squadron. But no matter how hard he tried, he couldn't picture that.

Across the restaurant, Shane rose and approached the table of Angry Angels, like a kid approaching a holo-film star. Her excitement built with each step she took.

"I just wanted to tell you all how much I admire and respect the 127th," she said to them, smiling.

One of the Angels, a woman with a hard jaw and even harder eyes, looked at Shane, mildly amused. "Thanks," she said. "We'll have four of your specials and a round of vita-pure."

The rest of the Angels snickered.

The look on Shane's face turned from admiration to humiliation to a deep, burning fury.

"She's not a waitress," said Nathan, coming up behind her.

The Angels bristled. People simply didn't talk to the Angry Angels in that tone of voice.

Nathan took a deep breath. He didn't care who they were. Shane didn't deserve to be treated like that. "She's a Marine," he told the hard woman. "Now apologize."

One of the other Angels stood. He looked much taller up close. Although Nathan felt intimidation digging into him like a fast-growing weed, he knew he couldn't back down now.

"Until she graduates she's slime," said the now *very* Angry Angel to Nathan. "And so are you. So now *you* apologize. If you know what's good for you."

The rest of the Angels stood in unison, a single fighting unit. Back at the recruits' table, Pags and the others watched in silence, not knowing what to do.

"Hey," said Shane, changing the tone of her voice, "what's the farthest you guys have flown?"

It seemed for a moment the tension had been broken. The hard-jawed woman grinned and boasted, "Four point eight light-years."

Shane grinned back. "Really? Well that's how far you can shove your apology."

What happened next was a fight for the books, because no one had ever taken on the Angry Angels. Nathan and Shane were outnumbered until Pags, Damphousse, and Wang finally joined in and it became an all-out brawl.

Cooper sat at the counter watching the show. A few stools down, McQueen was also watching. It almost seemed as if they were mimicking each other.

Cooper had mixed feelings about what he was seeing. Part of him felt like he wasn't about to go in there and help. Another, less familiar part of him felt like he *should* do something. They were—if not his friends—his Squadron, after all.

Cooper made a move to get up. So did McQueen. They looked at each other and reached a quiet understanding. They were probably the best fighters on either side, and they knew it. They knew, too, that their efforts would cancel each other out—and there was no reason to escalate this further than it had already gone. They both sat back down and kept out of it.

It took only a short time for the recruits to get beaten by the Angry Angels. But they were beaten as a team, as a unit. In its own way, it was a victory. The fight could have gone on until there was nothing left of them, if an emergency satellite feed hadn't suddenly taken over the video wall.

One by one they stopped fighting. The weary but imposing face of Spencer Chartwell, the President of the United Nations, was addressing the world with a desperation no one had ever seen him display.

Shane helped Nathan up from the floor. The roar in the restaurant settled as President Chartwell brought his dark tidings to the world.

"Not since the moment of creation has our universe changed so infinitely, so desperately, so quickly," Chartwell began.

Silence rapidly fell around the restaurant. Each Marine, both recruit and veteran, braced themselves for bad news.

"Tonight," Chartwell continued, "for the first time in the brief history of mankind, we are truly of one planet. Last evening, we confirmed that the landing party of the Tellus colony was massacred, unprovoked, by an advanced Alien civilization of tremendous force."

To Nathan, it was like a stab in the chest—sudden, sharp, and violent. The news rang through his head and echoed in every part of his body, until every muscle felt weak.

"Two hundred twenty-five are dead," announced Chartwell. "Twenty-five still unaccounted for."

"My God," said Shane. She turned to Nathan. She could see in his face there was something very personal about this news, something he had not shared with her or any of the others.

"We have only now learned that the Vesta colony suffered the same fate," Chartwell went on. "The Alien civilization has not responded to our attempts at communication. We know nothing of this race. Our only clue is the bloodshed they have left behind."

The Angry Angels were the first to take action, even before Chartwell was finished speaking. First McQueen and then the others made a determined path out the door, already preparing their minds for war.

"My fellow citizens of Earth," said Chartwell, in a desperate appeal to all mankind. "No matter where you stand on this planet, storm clouds of war gather over our home. We must stand together against the deluge, for we cannot possibly retreat. There is no moving the Earth."

Then Chartwell's face disappeared from the screen.

The Marines still left in the restaurant were reeling and uncertain in the silence that followed. The air in the room suddenly seemed almost as thin as the vacuum of space. Some, following the lead of the 127th, quickly left to return to the base. Others looked to each other for direction. Cooper returned to his dinner, trying to pretend, if only for a moment more, that nothing had changed.

Nathan, unable to catch his breath, his legs weak, pushed past the others. He stumbled out the back door into a dank alley filled with trash and ruined chairs, broken in earlier brawls. He was already trying to calculate the odds, clinging to the faint hope that Kylen might still be alive. Twenty-five colonists were unaccounted for. If they were still alive somewhere, there was a chance that Kylen might be one of them.

Nathan reached into his shirt, pulling out the phototag Kylen had thrown to him before they sealed the door of the ship. "I believe in you," she had told him. But was he strong enough to believe in himself, in the face of this new dark menace?

Aliens! Powerful and murderous. It was still too hard to believe—too much to accept.

The picture in his hand showed the two of them, smiling, during a happier time not too long ago, when a simple belief in each other was all it took to power them to distant stars.

Reality was harsher than either one of them could

have realized. Nathan gripped the phototag tightly in his palm, as if he could bring Kylen back by the mere strength of his grip. Up above, a night sky that once seemed glorious and inviting now twinkled with cold, unfeeling pinpoints of light—a billion hostile stars, threatening the end of the world.

Chapter 7

"FROM THIS MOMENT UNTIL WE WIN THIS WAR, THE ONLY EASY DAY . . . IS YESTERDAY!"

These were the last words the recruits heard Bougus fire at them before they were kicked out of the nest and into space for their final training mission.

The nuts and bolts of their training was the same, but ever since the Tellus massacre, there was a new intensity to what they were doing, an urgency—the urgency of war.

Their final training mission was to take place on Mars. It was a survival exercise coupled with the repair of a tracking station. And although the cargo ship that would take them on their long journey to Mars kept them as close together as an old-time submarine's crew, it couldn't block out the loneliness of space.

For weeks they had trained together, slowly becoming human weapons, focused and full of purpose. But as for being a team—that part was slower in coming. Perhaps because each of them had very different things on their minds.

Nathan focused his thoughts out of the ship's tiny window, searching for Tellus in the bright spray of stars. He was finally in space, but it was not the way he had dreamed it would be.

Cooper, on the other hand, occupied his mind with the practical matters at hand. He grumbled about the one-week supply of food, air, and water for the mission. He definitely had no love of the waste collection device in his spacesuit, which blinked a happy yellow light each time it was full. It had never occurred to him that a spacesuit would also be an interplanetary diaper. One, two, three, four, I love the Marine Corps.

Of the three of them, it was Shane who was best able to keep her thoughts directed on the mission. For her, the war that loomed on the horizon filled her with purpose and that faint whisper of destiny.

She listened while the rest lay on their bunks, all of them wondering about the future.

"I heard they've got an army of six million," said a grunt named Walker, usually one of the quieter members of the twelve-man Squadron.

Pags leaned up on one elbow and offered a half-hearted smile. "Come on, it can't be that one-sided," he said. "I mean, they can't have better planes than we do. . . ." Suddenly he didn't seem so sure. "Can they?"

The truth was, the Alien planes had to be more advanced. Everyone knew it.

"I knew we weren't alone," whispered Damp-

housse, "but I never thought it would be like this."
She turned to Pags, who still fought hard to keep his
ever-hopeful outlook. "Do you think you'd be scared
if you saw one?" she asked him.

Pags couldn't answer.

"I remember when I saw my first AI," mumbled
Wang. "They looked so human. But something inside me could tell. . . ."

"I felt that way when I saw my first In-Vitro,"
chimed in Damphousse, then realized a moment too
late what she had said. She turned to look at Cooper,
who silently lay on his bunk, staring up at the worn,
graphite ceiling.

"I . . . didn't mean that the way it sounded,
Coop," she said, and then looked away.

Shane watched for Cooper's reaction. What
Damphousse said must have hurt him, but he
seemed so cold, so unreachable. *When you get hurt
that much, that often,* thought Shane, *maybe you
just get used to it. Or worse—maybe in some strange
way, it becomes almost comfortable.*

Cooper rolled over on his bunk and closed his
eyes, as if the insult had been a good-night kiss from
the mother he never had.

While the others slept, Cooper Hawkes lay awake on
his uncomfortable bunk, trying to make sense of his
feelings. Rage was the only emotion that had ever
done him any good, so he had never bothered much

with the others. But over the past few weeks, he had sensed new feelings starting to take root in unexpected places. Like an inexplicable sort of protectiveness toward some of the others—like Wang and Pags, who often seemed like lost puppies. Not that he actually went out of his way to look out for them—but part of him wanted to.

And then there was Shane. He found himself watching her more and more often, wanting to say something to her that wasn't crude or obnoxious, but not daring to.

What was wrong with him anyway? This wasn't like him.

In the bunk beside him, Shane suddenly tossed and turned in the throes of a nightmare. Cooper went over to her, not sure what to do. It reminded him of the time he blew a coolant injector on an Earthspeeder he had stolen. There, by the side of the road, he had popped its smooth hood to find an impossibly complicated engine, and he had had no idea what to do with it.

He reached out and gently shook Shane awake. She let out a cry but then turned to look at him, the terror in her eyes quickly fading with the dream.

"Sorry I woke you," she said to him.

Cooper shrugged. "Wasn't asleep."

She propped herself up and took a long look into Cooper's eyes. To his own amazement, Cooper allowed it.

"Don't take this wrong," Shane said, "but . . . is it true that In-Vitros can't dream?"

He wanted to hate her for asking a question like that, but instead he felt grateful that she had. "I dream," he answered. "I never had parents, but I always dream about them."

Shane nodded. "Me too," she said, and explained to him how she saw them executed in the AI War. She showed him the scar where her sister had bitten her hand.

Cooper took her hand to look at it. He didn't feel the scar—but he did feel how soft and warm her hand was.

"All these years I took care of my sisters," Shane explained. "But I had to get away from taking care of people. That's why I joined the Corps. I don't want to take care of anyone for a while. Does that sound bad?"

Cooper looked up. Her eyes were still looking at him—looking *into* him. He knew he should have hated that feeling, but he liked it. And he didn't know what to do about it.

"Did you—did you ever lose anyone?" asked Shane.

Before he knew what he was doing, or even why he was doing it, Cooper found himself reaching behind Shane's neck and pulling her close. And kissing her.

It wasn't like the kisses he had given other girls

on his jagged journey through life. Unlike the others, this kiss had a feeling attached.

The kiss lasted only an instant before Shane clubbed him in fine military fashion and pushed him back on his bunk.

"What the heck was that?" she asked. She didn't seem angry, merely amused.

Cooper, on the other hand, was furious. Not at her. Her reaction made perfect sense. He was angry at himself. He had always understood his actions so very well—but now that was all falling apart. He couldn't explain to himself—much less to her—why he'd done it. And if it was an apology she wanted, she wasn't going to get one. Apologies were something he simply didn't do.

"I don't know much about loss and nightmares," he said snidely, "so don't get in an uproar." He climbed back in his bunk but still kept his eyes on her, staring coldly, to make sure *she* was the one who felt uncomfortable.

"I won't be around much longer anyway," he added.

And only when she finally turned away from him in anger did he relax.

Nathan was the first one off the transport, firmly planting his foot in the crimson dust of Mars. The print he left behind reminded him of that famous photo of the first footprint on the moon.

Though his flightsuit was fully pressurized, Nathan felt his breath taken away by the expansive red landscape around him.

Cooper, on the other hand, was not impressed.

"What? Are you looking to buy real estate? Let's get this over with!" Cooper said, already unloading gear.

The group looked at Nathan and at Cooper, not quite sure who was giving the orders.

Nathan stood firm on the Martian soil. "First we secure our position."

"Our position is out in the middle of nowhere," mocked Cooper. "There, secured." He turned to the others. "Now unload this gear!"

Nathan wasn't about to take this kind of disrespect from Cooper. While Nathan was never officially made leader of the squad, Bougus had always left him in charge during the flight simulations and many of the other exercises.

But everyone was painfully aware that Bougus was now on another planet. They were on their own for this mission.

Nathan grabbed Cooper and turned him around.

"The manual states—" Nathan began, but Cooper just laughed.

"The manual? When they drop you in the middle of a hairy fur ball, you're gonna go checking the manual?" Cooper shook his head in disgust. "That's right, follow their rules. Let them keep bossing you around."

Suddenly, Nathan couldn't take it anymore. There were plenty of times back on Earth when Nathan had wanted to punch Cooper's head through a wall, but he had held back. He was a Marine, and he had discipline, even if this sorry Tank didn't. But in this strange new environment without the eyes of the Marine Corps upon him, Nathan found that he couldn't control himself. He charged at Cooper, fists flying.

Cooper, who had the sharpened battle instincts of an alley cat, blocked Nathan's punch—and countered. Cooper's padded fist caught Nathan in the stomach and sent him flying—much further than it would have in Earth's heavier gravity.

In an instant, they were both on the ground, swinging at one another furiously. Forgetting the fact that they were geared up for the atmosphere of Mars, they punched the delicate equipment of each other's suits, butting their heavy glass and steel helmets like two rams.

A red cloud of dust rose into the air around them, until finally Shane tore them apart.

"What is wrong with you two? Knock it off!" She stared them down. "We're not gonna blow our mission because you jerks feel like fighting. Got that?"

Nathan and Cooper wouldn't look at each other, or at her.

"We're pushing on," she continued, "so you'd better get your heads screwed on straight."

Shane had defused a tense situation, quickly and

effectively. Like a leader. Suddenly everyone in the group was looking at her.

"Damphousse, tell West our position," she ordered.

A long silent moment passed. Shane looked to Nathan and Cooper on the ground, and to the others. When it came down to it, there was no question who the real leader was in this group. Whether or not anyone wanted to admit it, Shane was the only one who could give orders that everyone would listen to.

Nathan could feel whatever control he had once had over the group completely slip away. He was surprised to find that for some reason, it didn't bother him. Perhaps that was part of Shane's leadership ability too.

"We're forty-five degrees south, two-hundred-and-seventy-one west; the Helles Planes," announced Damphousse at last. "The tracking drone is about four clicks from here."

"Okay," said Shane. "Grab your gear; let's move out."

They all fell in behind her and headed off across the Martian sands. Everyone but Cooper, who still sat in the sand, forgotten as usual.

His air mix had been set low to conserve oxygen. The fight had taken a lot out of him. He was still catching his breath when he looked up and saw a hand in his face.

It was Pags, offering to help him up. Cooper thought he sensed pity, and it just made him mad.

"I can get up myself."

"Probably," said Pags, "but it looks like you could use a hand, and I'm offering one."

Again Cooper was visited by a feeling that was strange and new to him. He thought it might be friendship. He reached out his hand and let Pags help him up.

"It ain't easy for me to recognize a helping hand," Cooper admitted to him.

"If that's a thank-you, don't worry about it," said Pags. "Someday you'll pay me back."

As they walked off together to join the others, Cooper idly began to wonder what his life might have been like had he been a full-fledged human instead of just a Tank. Maybe, in a better world, he would have had a younger brother like Pags.

It must have been a sandstorm that destroyed the tracking station they were sent to repair. When they reached it, they found the device was eroded and dented, its solar-array foil flapping in the thin, carbon-dioxide wind.

They set to work replacing the transceiver. Now more than ever, every tracking station was needed—even one as small and outdated as this one.

Halfway through the repair, Damphousse pulled out a small golden disk from the antiquated machine.

"Oh wow," said Wang. "An Earth message." He turned to the others. "Back in the twenty-first century it was required that all off-Earth installations have one of these. It has pictures and sounds of Earth, just in case an extraterrestrial happened to wander on by."

The others laughed. Wang was always claiming that his family had been key players in the presuperconductor computer revolution a few hundred years ago, so it was only natural that he would know all about this stuff.

He took the little gold disk and inserted it into what must have been the disk drive. Music played thinly into the diffuse Martian air. It was something every Earthling could recognize.

"Mozart," said Nathan. "Concerto in D."

Shane shook her head sadly. "If only this could have been our first contact with the Aliens."

Cooper reached over and changed the tracks. Suddenly the sound of bagpipes filled the air.

Pags laughed. "And if they heard this, they would have wiped us out a long time ago."

Cooper switched tracks again, and something strange but rhythmic blasted through the air, heavy on percussion and guitar.

"What the heck is that?" Damphousse laughed.

"I know this," said Pags. "I studied it once in music appreciation. They called it rock and roll. This group is called, uh, the Pink Floyd. Yeah, that's it."

Everyone figured he probably made it up, but it sounded just bizarre enough to fit the late twentieth century.

Pags spread his legs apart, pretended his blaster was an electric guitar, and began to wildly strum it to the music, bouncing and gyrating like he was being electrocuted. He looked funny enough to get even Cooper to laugh.

But their laughter didn't last long.

BOOM! A sound that could only be a sonic blast echoed from above. With a flash of light, a fiery streak arced across the sky. Vanishing behind a volcano's summit, the flying object hit the ground with another bright flash.

Shane was the only one with the presence of mind to start counting, measuring the seconds until the sound of the impact reached them. *BOOM!* The ground beneath their feet shook with an explosion more ominous than thunder.

Shane calculated the difference between the speed of sound on Earth and Mars. She looked up at the others. "About ten miles away."

"It was too slow for a meteor," said Nathan.

No one was willing to guess what it might be.

"Should some of us check it out?" asked Wang, clearly hoping the answer would be no.

"We'll all go," said Shane, deciding quickly.

"Great. Let's do it," shouted Pags with his usual enthusiasm.

Shane led the way, and they trekked into the Martian sunset.

This war between the worlds will
be fought on a new battlefield—
Space: Above and Beyond.

Kylen Celina and Nathan West—
star-crossed lovers.

The advanced tools of war
used by the Alien army—
triple-winged fighters so black
they almost disappear against
the deadness of space.

The 2nd Air Wing, 58th Squadron—
ready for battle in the stars.

Cooper Hawkes and Shane Vansen
come from completely different
backgrounds. Can they put their
differences aside and join forces
to defend the Earth?

The 58th Squadron's first
close encounter with the enemy

McQueen would carry the scars
of the vicious Alien attack
for the rest of his life.

Hide-and-seek may seem like a
game, but not when you're playing
in an asteroid belt!

Chapter 8

They walked toward a sunset so red it seemed painted in blood. But by the time they reached the blast site, the crimson sky had turned blacker than any night on Earth. Shane arrived first, and the others followed her lead as she hunched apprehensively behind a sand-molded outcropping of rock.

Before them lay the wreck of something entirely unfamiliar, still glowing with the heat of its violent descent. Sharp and jagged, it was hard to believe it was something of human design.

"Could be a Mars orbiter," Shane suggested.

"Maybe it's a classified recon ship," Wang offered.

Shane could feel anticipation and fear building in everyone around her. She could feel it welling up inside herself, but she beat it down.

"Damphousse, West, Walker, Pags—let's move in and take a look. The rest of you spread out and provide cover," she ordered.

Everyone began to move. Everyone, that is, except for Cooper. He had kept quiet for most of the trek. He had even decided to accept Shane's authority without grumbling about it. But why hadn't she called him to explore the craft as well?

"You want me to go?" he asked, matter-of-factly, as if perhaps Shane had just forgotten to call his name.

Shane shook her head. "You stay here," she told him, quietly, "in case something happens."

Cooper accepted this without further word. He didn't know if it was some sort of punishment for his attitude, or a position of honor. Either way, Cooper had never liked the idea of staying put.

The others fell out, moving clumsily but quickly in their padded suits. Their M-190 rifles were drawn and aimed at the strange craft. They had no idea what to expect.

"Radiation levels?" Shane asked Walker. From the quick clicks she could hear coming from his Geiger counter, she didn't really need an answer.

"Uh, let's just say we don't stay long," said Walker.

With half the platoon covering them, Shane advanced her group toward the craft. As they got closer they could feel the heat through their thermal suits. Even in the dark, it was clear that the craft was beyond the technology of even the most classified military experiments.

"What *is* it?" asked Damphousse.

They all knew what it had to be, but no one dared say out loud.

Nathan pushed forward, peering into a huge hole in its hull. There was an angry exhilaration in him now. How far had this thing come? Could it have been at Tellus? Could it have been part of that brutal massacre?

"I can't see a cockpit or anything," Nathan said.

There didn't even seem to be a hint of electronics within the hull. Nathan grabbed on to the edge of the hole, preparing to go further inside.

Above him, something moved.

Heavy and black, it fell from the darkness above, striking him on the shoulder. Instinctively, he knew it was one of *them*. An Alien!

Nathan lurched back and spun around hearing a few gasps in his earpiece, and something else: the clatter of weapons being raised.

The shock was enough to fill them all with a powerful adrenaline rush. A heavily armored creature lay at Nathan's feet. Even in the inky night, he could tell the creature was not moving. He was the first to raise his flashlight and shine it at the thing. It was definitely dead.

The spacesuit it wore betrayed a shape far from human: clawed feet, long taloned fingers, a massive, oversized head, and a sharp protrusion in the center of its chest.

It was their first glimpse of the enemy.

Far back, Cooper Hawkes watched, still brooding, barely able to see but hearing the voices in his communicator. When he saw the object fall and the way they had all jumped back, he knew it had to be an Alien. He cursed Shane for not letting him be a part of the action, and watched the hole closely.

Too closely.

He had been assigned the job of watching the big picture—of keeping a wide eye open so they'd know if there was any danger. He realized an instant too late that he wasn't looking wide enough.

BOOM! A blast came from behind the ship—a bright yellow pulse of light that hit Pags in the chest and threw him back ten feet.

"Pags!" screamed Cooper, as if screaming his name could do anything. He raised his weapon as the platoon scattered, shouting wildly at one another.

Shane tried to order commands, but the chaos left no room for any sort of sensible response.

BOOM! BOOM! More blasts—in all directions now. It was an ambush. It seemed like a hundred of the Aliens were surrounding them, shooting.

But soon it became clear that most of the blasts were coming from their own weapons, pulverizing stone and raising heavy clouds of red dust that added to the confusion.

As the shooting slowed, a shadow raced out from behind the Alien ship. Despite its huge head and long arms, it was moving impossibly fast.

The small squadron of Marines could hardly believe their eyes. There was only one Alien, but with a single weapon far more powerful than all of theirs combined. The superpowered gun fired blinding light mortars and left holes in the Martian rock three feet deep.

Without waiting for Shane's order, the Marines opened fire on the thing, but its armor seemed unaffected by the platoon's blasts.

Then the Alien took aim at Shane.

BOOM! Nathan barely saw the blast as the rocket zoomed past him. It clipped Shane's suit and threw her to the ground. Nathan watched in horror as she squirmed in the red dust.

But she hadn't been hit! The blast only blew her air regulator. Nathan could see the tube swinging free— pumping her oxygen into the thin, deadly Martian atmosphere. With the air sucked from her suit and lungs, it would only take seconds for her to die.

Dodging the bright yellow blasts crisscrossing before him, Nathan raced to her. Locking out his own life support, he freed his oxygen tube. He jammed it into the hole in Shane's helmet. Then, connected like Siamese twins, he hobbled with her behind a rock, praying that the Alien didn't have a clear shot at them. Otherwise, they'd both be dead.

Twenty yards away, Cooper was still in the best position for the battle. No matter where the thing tried to hide, Cooper found it in his digital gun sights and opened fire. Every bullet ricocheted off the creature's armor, but it was still affected by the blasts.

BANG! BANG! One shot threw the creature's shoulder back, another made it stumble. Now it was moving slower, almost hobbling. Cooper had weakened it! Finally, it stumbled behind a boulder where Cooper couldn't get a bead on it.

In the clear, Cooper hurried down to where Nathan and Damphousse huddled over Shane, frantically working on her suit. He'd seen her get hit and suspected the worst.

"She's dead, isn't she?" he heard himself say.

For an instant there was only static in reply. Then he heard her through his earpiece, loud and clear. "No such luck, Hawkes."

When Damphousse and Nathan stepped back, he could see the jury-rigged repairs to her regulator.

He wanted to say, Glad you're okay, or something like that. But he held back.

The Alien had stopped firing.

Nathan was the first to straighten up and take stock of their position. He took a good look at his targeting computer, found the creature's life signs, and took off after it, solo.

"West!" shouted Shane. "Get back here!"

But Nathan wasn't about to stop and argue.

With the platoon trying to catch up with him, Nathan tracked the Alien's unnatural life signs.

A single blast from extremely close range shook the boulder behind him. Nathan quickly took cover, then aimed at the thing, now just a few meters away. As the Alien began to raise its weapon, pointed right at Nathan, the others came around both sides of the rock, their M-190s trained on it.

To everyone's surprise, the Alien put its weapon down and simply crouched there on misshapen knees.

"I think it's trying to surrender," said Wang.

One by one they all lowered their weapons. Everyone, that is, but Nathan.

At this close range, Nathan wanted to just open fire on the creature, blasting it again and again and again. He knew he wouldn't be satisfied until its stinking hide was dead—as dead as the first one they had come across. It took all of his willpower to lower his weapon, but he did.

Back in the shadow of the ruined Alien craft, Damphousse knelt beside a single human body stretched out on its back.

In the dim light, it was hard to tell if the body was covered in blood, or in red Martian sand. But Cooper knew whose body it had to be.

Damphousse looked up sadly at her comrades. "Pags is dead."

Cooper found himself kneeling over Pags, staring into the blackened wound in his friend's chest, too angry to scream.

Chapter 9

There was no lack of volunteers willing to guard the creature once they got back to the transport. In fact, more than half of their platoon kept their weapons raised, as if the thing might, at any moment, leap out of the corner and chew through all of them.

In the pressurized transport, with their helmets off, they found the creature's stench almost unbearable. They must have put a hole in its armor somewhere.

"It smells sulfuric," suggested Shane. The rotten-egg smell had them all breathing through their mouths.

"It must be a scout," mused Damphousse. "It was probably headed to Earth but didn't make it."

"I'll bet it sent a distress call," added Wang.

Shane agreed. "There'll definitely be more coming."

Cooper ventured closer to the Alien. They had tightly tied its talon hands together with heavy synthrope. Now those angry-looking claws trembled. Perhaps from the temperature. Perhaps from fear.

Cooper put down his rifle weapon and raised his hands as he approached the creature, so it knew he wasn't going to hurt it—at least not then.

"Don't!" shouted Shane. "What if it carries some disease . . ."

"Vansen, you sound like the mother I never had," Cooper said as he continued his advance.

He took a good, close look at the thing. "That's a pretty thick armored flight suit."

"Or one heck of an exoskeleton," suggested Wang.

The truth was, they knew so little about it, they couldn't tell what was flesh and what was clothing. Cooper saw something metallic clipped on to the strange finlike ridge in its chest.

He reached tentatively and pulled it off. The creature tried to lurch forward against its bonds, wailing in a hollow screech that echoed in the metal chamber.

"Maybe it's a key," offered Damphousse, looking at the thin metal bar, "or some sort of encoded information."

Cooper held it out in front of the creature. "What is this?" he demanded.

The creature struggled against its binds. Trying to remain cool, Cooper grabbed his handgun. As far as he was concerned, diplomacy was always best backed up with a gun to the head.

He jammed the gun against the side of the creature's helmet, right between two joints where a bullet was sure to get through.

"*What is it?*" Cooper demanded again.

The creature slowly turned and nodded toward Nathan.

"What?" asked Cooper, surprised. "What about him?"

Maneuvering with the rope tying its hands, it aimed a long finger at the phototag hanging around Nathan's neck. Cooper looked at the small Alien device in his hand, then at the phototag.

"You mean . . . this . . . is that?"

The creature nodded, slowly.

"It nodded," Shane commented. "It knows some of our gestures."

"It knows about us," remarked Damphousse, "but we know nothing about it."

Wang took a look at the Alien device. "So it must be a picture of its family or something."

They all turned to the creature and tried to imagine this thing having a family. As monstrous as it was, and no matter what it had done to Pags, they couldn't help but begin to feel a touch of compassion for it.

Except Nathan. When he looked at it, all he could see was its blaster aimed at Kylen's head. *Could it have been involved in the attack on Tellus*? he wondered. Could it be pointing at his phototag because it recognized Kylen's face? No, he had no sympathy for this monster.

Shane took the Alien's photocell from Cooper and put it into the creature's bound claws. Its talons clutched it tightly.

"Maybe we ought to give it some water," Wang suggested.

Damphousse grabbed her canteen. "Right. That's probably one of the only things we have in common."

This was more than Nathan could stand. "What is wrong with all of you?" he shouted. "We're low on rations! And you're gonna waste water on that . . . that *thing*? No way!"

Nathan raised his M-190, pointing at the Alien's head. The creature lurched against its ties, this time backward instead of forward, clearly terrified.

"This thing killed Pags!" Nathan screamed, as he tightened his finger on the trigger. "Who knows how many others it's killed."

Nathan knew that at this close range, he'd be able to blast the creature's head wide open, no matter how strong its body armor. But as much as he wanted to, he couldn't make himself pull the trigger. He didn't know why.

Unable to stand the smell in his nostrils or the fire in his head a moment longer, Nathan grabbed his helmet and stormed out the airlock.

When he was gone, Damphousse raised her canteen again. "Well, I'm giving it some water," she announced. "Any other objections?"

There was a brief silence.

"Go ahead," said Shane.

"Let's show it what it means to be human."

As Damphousse approached, the Alien turned to her, looking over the canteen curiously. Then it cocked its head. Beneath the armor was soft gray flesh, broken by three slits, like gills.

"That must be its mouth," said Wang, trying to hide his disgust.

It tilted its head further, leaning toward Damphousse and the nozzle of the canteen. She inserted the nozzle into one of the gills.

Slurp. Slurp. Damphousse could feel the weight of the canteen lighten as the thing sucked it dry in a matter of seconds.

The Alien sat still for a moment. Suddenly, it began to shake and lurch violently from side to side. Damphousse jumped back, unsure of what was happening. Cooper raised his weapon again. They all stared in horror as thick, green bile exploded from the creature's mouth. A phosphorescent slimy ooze, thick and putrid, poured down its black armor and onto the cabin floor.

The creature lurched just one more time. Its pained wails faded to a weak gurgle as its head fell forward and its hands went limp. The Marines stood silently staring at it, realizing that the only thing that these Aliens and humans had in common was death.

They dragged its body out and laid it next to Pags, whom they had carried all the way back from the crash site.

"Did we kill it?" Damphousse asked, "or did it kill itself?"

It was Walker, the youngest now that Pags was dead, who said, "I've never even seen a dead body before today."

"Don't worry," offered Cooper with his usual cynicism. "It won't be the last."

Nathan leaned down to examine the Alien one last time. He had wanted to kill it, but now its death held no satisfaction for him. Its claws still clutched the Alien card, he noticed. Nathan could see no picture in it, just a black square. But then, maybe the creature didn't see in white light. The picture could very well be an infrared or ultraviolet image. Whatever it was, it belonged to the creature. Nathan pulled the picture from the dead Alien's claws and secured it back onto the creature's chest.

Around them the carbon-dioxide wind howled like the voices of the dead, both human and Alien.

Chapter 10

Arlington National Cemetery hadn't changed much in two hundred years. Somehow, there was always more room for the honored dead.

Dressed in their full military dress uniforms, the Marine unit now known as the 58th Space Cavalry Squadron stood at attention at Mike Pagodin's funeral.

Cooper stood there, feeling the tight collar chafe the gestation navel on the back of his neck. He wanted to say something to Pags's parents. But no words were good enough.

Nathan and Shane rose to fold the flag that was draped over Pags's coffin. They handed the flag to Pags's mother with a solemn, respectful nod.

They all felt responsible for Pags's death. Cooper because he should have been watching better. Shane because she was the one who'd led them to the Alien's ship. And Nathan because he was the one nearest to Pags when the deadly blast came.

Pags wasn't the first one to die in this war, but he was the first of the dead to come home. And in a war where the future seemed so bleak, each of the Marines wondered how they could go on without Pags's enthusiasm and boundless optimism.

As the coffin was gently lowered into the ground, a row of seven Marines fired off a twenty-one-gun salute into the glorious Earth sunset—a sunset that few of them might ever see again.

The war was real. Pags's death brought home to every one of the new recruits that they weren't recruits anymore. They were full-fledged Marines, pilots who were about to launch themselves into an interstellar battle more violent and deadly than any Earth war had ever been.

Nathan, Shane, Cooper, Damphousse, Wang, and the rest of the Squadron stood in one of the immense hangars on Loxley Base. There was no more training to go through, no more drills to endure. Nothing was before them now but war.

"Today you have been assigned your SA-43 Endo/Exo-Atmospheric Attack Jets."

Sergeant Major Bougus's voice was commanding and firm but somehow not as powerful as it had been before. He seemed tired, weakened in some way. Like the Marine Corps itself. The rumor was that every Squadron sent out to battle had suffered major casualties. It was enough to make the hardiest of Marines begin to lose heart.

"Your current orders are to take forty-eight-hours' leave," Bougus proclaimed.

The order surprised them all.

"Sir, ship us out, sir!" Nathan shouted. Even as he stood there in the hangar, Nathan already felt he had left the Earth behind. His place was out there. If he couldn't be with Kylen, then at least he would die fighting the creatures who had murdered her.

"Sir," Shane asked, "why have we been on accelerated training if we're not going to be used, sir?"

Bougus strode forward as if he were about to get into Shane's face and ask her to drop and give him fifty. But instead he stopped short and hesitated. His eyes swept across each of them.

"Other than what you found on Mars, we have no idea what lies ahead," Bougus confessed to them. "We know basically nothing about the enemy—numbers, weapons, tactics." As he spoke, they could see the anger in him, the frustration rising in his voice. "That is why we have been losing—and losing badly—in every battle of this war."

He made eye contact with Nathan and then with Shane.

"Don't be in such a hurry," he advised them.

The meaning of his words cut clear to the bone.

"Go see your families. It could be for the last time."

The seasoned Marine eyed them, masking any emotions he might have had, then gave them a crisp salute.

They all returned the salute in perfect unity, just

as Bougus had trained them to do—as a team.

Bougus dismissed them, and the two lines of Marines fell out of formation, back to being just individuals with only two days to make peace with the life they had led on Earth.

All the others had places to go. Cooper Hawkes had no family and no home to speak of. When the other members of his unit had dispersed, Cooper wandered around the hangar. The SA-43 Attack Jets around him were sleek and fast, aerodynamically designed for atmospheric battle, yet fitted with dozens of delicate thrusters to give them perfect maneuverability in deep space. The angle of their wings cut forward, and at the nose smaller wings jutted out, filled with micro-thrusters that helped give the pilot the sensation of aerodynamic flight even without the luxury of an atmosphere. The jet's flat wide nose made it look just like a hammerhead shark. They were aptly nicknamed "Hammerheads."

Cooper approached one of the Hammerheads, one with the insignia of the Angry Angels painted on its nose. McQueen knelt on the wing, leaning into the cockpit, preparing his fighter for battle. Cooper tried to imagine himself in a plane, tearing across empty space toward certain death. He tried to imagine himself taking his own Hammerhead into battle against a thousand enemy ships like the one he saw on Mars. His imagination couldn't take him that far.

Sure, he had been through hundreds of simulations. And although the simulators were reported to be identical to flying the real thing, there was one key element missing. You didn't die when your simulator blew up.

"I'll never get in one of those," Cooper announced to McQueen.

McQueen didn't turn to him.

"Ten of us Tanks were with the Tellus colony," McQueen said.

Cooper nodded. McQueen confirmed something he'd suspected all along. The man was far too cold, too distant, to be anything but a Tank. He wondered how many years McQueen had spent scraping through life and scavenging in dark alleys before winding up here, one of the most respected pilots in the Corps.

Cooper tried to imagine himself respected. He couldn't picture that either, so he thought of the Tanks who died at Tellus.

Then he thought of all the flesh-born humans who had taunted him and beat him all his life. Finally he thought of his new comrades, who still didn't entirely trust him.

"I'm not going to die for them," Cooper said out loud.

McQueen turned to him.

"Then what *would* you die for?" he asked.

Cooper looked away. A wave of anger laced with sadness wove its way through him. He didn't know what was worth dying for. And that made him feel less than human.

Chapter 11

Shane could have gone out to California to spend the time with her sisters. After all, it was just an hour mag-lev ride from Loxley, Alabama, even with the change in Dallas. But they had fought so bitterly before Shane left. She knew they didn't want to see her. To them Shane had become like a parent they had to grow away from. She had already said her good-byes to them months ago and had been through that pain. No need to open the wounds again now.

So naturally she said yes when Nathan invited her to see his family.

"I don't know if my folks even want to see me," Nathan told her. "I never told them I was joining the Corps."

Together they took a mag-lev under the American heartland, then a surface transport to a farmhouse nestled amid the green foothills of the Rocky Mountains.

It looked so perfect to Shane. It was everything she wished her childhood home could have been: peaceful and safe, surrounded by beauty and the ever-present aroma of roses and gardenias.

But to Nathan the sights and smells had a far different meaning. It wasn't the joy of childhood that filled him but the pain of all he had lost. He had dreamed of being an explorer, but instead he had turned into a soldier. He had dreamed of a life with Kylen, but now, he would probably only join her in death.

He looked at the tangle of woods where he used to play laser tag with his friends. That was back when blasters were just toys and wars were just exciting stories from long ago and far away.

The boy he had been was gone now, and yet he still had a hard time thinking of himself as a man. Especially now. Especially here.

The front door swung open. A boy stood in the doorway. For a strange moment, Nathan thought he saw himself standing there, fourteen and wide-eyed, filled with all the wonder of the universe.

It only took a moment for him to realize it was John, his youngest brother. It looked like he'd grown six inches in the months that Nathan had been away.

"Nathan?" said John, clearly thrown by the fact that Nathan was wearing a uniform. Then he turned and shouted into the house. "Mom! Dad! It's Nathan!"

Nathan and Shane took a step forward as his parents came out to greet them. John leaped into Nathan's arms for a hug, just as he had always done when he was younger. But Mr. and Mrs. West kept their distance.

There seemed such a gap between them now, filled with all the things that Nathan had never told them. Finally he crossed that distance, giving his mother a hug, his father a firm handshake.

"Mom, Dad," Nathan said. "This is my friend, Shane Vansen."

Shane grinned and shook their hands.

"It's a pleasure, Mr. and Mrs. West."

Mrs. West smiled halfheartedly. "Dinner's almost ready," she said, and turned to head back into the house, trying to hide the tears that were welling up in her eyes.

Nathan was unable to hold his father's gaze. He turned to John. "I was gonna give you a rock I pocketed on Mars, but they took it."

"Come on inside," Mr. West said. He gripped Nathan's shoulder, giving his son the same look he'd given him long ago when Nathan had told him about being accepted into the colonization program. A look of overwhelming worry.

"Neil, can't you find something else to watch?" Mrs. West wouldn't even look at the war reports anymore, which was hard to do since the TV took up an entire wall.

"Come on, Mom," said Neil, the middle brother, seventeen and also the spitting image of Nathan. "You can't pretend it's not happening."

"And anyway," John added, "it's on all eight hundred stations."

Mrs. West busied herself programming the oven. "I sincerely doubt that," she said.

With all the introductions made, Shane sat between John and Neil, feeling more comfortable there than with her own sisters. She envied Nathan his family, yet his own discomfort with them filled the air more strongly than the smell of his mother's cooking.

As for Nathan, he chose to keep his thoughts to himself as he watched the war reports beside Shane and his brothers. Even out here, hundreds of miles from the nearest military base, Nathan felt the war surround him.

On the TV screen, a reporter stationed at Vandenberg Air Force Base shouted above the roar of the wind and soaring fighters. Military personnel ran determinedly around her as she spoke of the mobilization and movements of the massive starcraft carriers in deep space.

"I heard the Alien fighters are made of an unknown metal," Neil said, turning down the volume, "and we can't harm them." The look on his face was a combination of excitement and terror. It sounded like he couldn't wait until he was old enough to fight himself.

Nathan turned to him, furious at the thought that

it could only be a few short months before his little brother was swept into the war as well.

"We've only just started reverse-engineering the ship we found," he said. "So anything you've heard is just rumor."

Neil shook his head. "But Kylen's brother told us—" He stopped short. The tension in the room increased.

The reason was clear to everyone there, except of course for Shane.

Who's Kylen? Shane wondered. From the very beginning Nathan had never shared much about his personal life. She had always assumed it was because he had nothing much to share: a normal, happy family living in an uneventful part of the world. Only now did she realize there was much more to Nathan than she had given him credit for.

Nathan stood and left the room, but not before reflexively grabbing the phototag he always wore around his neck. It didn't take a gene surgeon to figure out that the girl in the picture must be Kylen. Shane wondered why her very name brought such ice to the room.

When Nathan was gone, Neil turned to Shane. "Anyway, he said that it doesn't seem like we can win."

On her other side, John leaned forward to see what Shane's response would be. After all, she and Nathan were their closest link to the war.

Shane *did* know something about the upcoming battle, enough to know there was far more hope than Neil thought.

She offered them a comforting smile. "Don't worry. This time out we'll beat them."

"How do you know?" John asked.

"Because," Shane said, "this time they're going up against the 127th—the *Angry Angels.* Those guys will knock the enemy into Andromeda."

John smiled broadly at the thought, but Neil could muster only a doubtful grin.

Mr. West had made himself scarce from the moment Nathan had arrived. Now Nathan found him on the back porch, staring out at the spectacular vista below.

Nathan let the screen door close loudly enough so his father would know he was there.

"Back during the time of the AI Wars," his father said, "I would stand here looking at these mountains, and they would comfort me, because somehow, deep down, I knew the war would never come here. That it would be fought in the cities, on the seas, and on the moon." His eyes changed as he scanned the mountain range, dark against the setting sun.

"But now as I look, I keep wondering how long until their ships come screaming over the mountains?"

"Just because they attacked us first, it doesn't

mean they're going to win." Nathan forced a smile. "Do you remember your twentieth-century history? Second World War. Pearl Harbor."

"We knew the enemy then," his father said. "They had two eyes and five fingers. They breathed the same air and died of the same wounds."

Nathan watched his father try to force back his emotions. "If you had to sign up, Nathan, why couldn't you have waited until we knew more about the enemy?"

Nathan felt his own emotions rising. He pounded the railing. "I had no choice!" he insisted.

"You could have talked to me. I could have pulled some strings."

Nathan threw up his hands. "With whom? Dad, I was under contract to the colony project. It was either join the military, or spend the next seven years of my life retraining for a different colony mission that I might not even get assigned to."

"You could have gotten out of that contract, and you know it!" his father shouted. "But you just had to get into space at all costs, didn't you?"

Nathan tried to control his anger. "If it was the only way I could get to Tellus, then yes, I would get there at all costs."

Mr. West looked at Nathan's face, as if he didn't know his son anymore.

"You can't possibly think that Kylen is still alive, Nathan."

"They reported twenty-five survivors before contact was lost."

His father shook his head. "Those aren't odds worth dying for."

Nathan looked away. It always amazed him, the ability his father had to put doubt in him. He could tell his father what he did on Mars, how he helped capture the first Alien, how crucial he had already been to the war effort. But his father would find a way to trivialize it and make Nathan feel even *that* had been a mistake.

"I'd give anything for the chance to fight with my father."

They both turned to see Shane stepping through the screen door. From the look on her face, Nathan could tell she had heard everything.

"I'll bet if he were alive," Shane continued, "he'd probably scream at me, too, for following in his footsteps and joining the Marines. He'd be so afraid for me, he might even forget to show me how proud he was."

Nathan turned to his father. It hadn't occurred to him that pride might fit somewhere in his father's mix of emotions. Nonetheless, now that he was looking, Nathan could see it there.

"Your friend's smarter than both of us," Mr. West said. Then he went inside.

When he was gone, Shane looked at Nathan with more curiosity than she had looked at anything on Mars.

"You were supposed to go to Tellus?"

Nathan shrugged. "Ancient history."

"Not so ancient," she corrected him.

The moment was as uncomfortable as it could be between friends. For Shane, it didn't feel quite like a betrayal. But to find out so much about someone you thought you knew, so quickly . . .

"You must have loved her very much," she said abruptly.

Nathan threw her a sharp look, as if she had said something awful. "I still do."

"Sorry."

She reached out and took hold of the phototag. "You look perfect together. People who look that perfect together don't stay apart for very long."

Nathan allowed himself a small grin. "Are you jealous, Lieutenant Vansen?"

Shane thought about it. Was she really? She didn't think so. After all, Nathan was just a friend. Although her feelings for him were strong, they didn't go beyond friendship. If she was jealous of something, it wasn't of Kylen. It was of them both—of what they had together. Shane was afraid she might never feel that close to someone, ever.

She kept her voice light. "Nah. You're not my type."

Nathan laughed, and Shane couldn't tell whether it was a laugh of disappointment or relief. In truth, it was a little bit of both.

"I want you to know something," she said. "When we get up there and beat these . . . monsters, I'll fly right beside you to Tellus and help you find her."

They weren't just words. She meant it and could tell that Nathan knew that—the same way she knew Nathan would follow her into battle and give his life if she gave the order.

Chapter 12

AWOL. Racing away from Loxley, Alabama, at thirty miles a minute, Cooper Hawkes fought to put it all behind him. Who would know? Who would care if he deserted? He would never see any of their faces ever again. They'd probably all be dead soon, anyway.

Not him. No, he was a survivor. From the way it looked, the world would pretty soon be overrun by those foul-smelling Aliens. And if that were true, it would be every man for himself, struggling to get by, hiding in every crevice the Earth had to offer.

Cooper didn't know much about war, but he did know about survival. And he knew that, right now, survival meant staying far, far away from the cockpit of a fighter jet.

Yet even though deep down he knew that running was the best way to survive, something about leaving his Squadron behind tore him up inside.

Nathan, Shane, the others—why couldn't he forget them? Why couldn't he flush them from his mind the way he had done in the past—with anyone and anything that got too close? In Cooper's experience, the only emotions that were useful were fury and fear. They were the tools of survival—the emotions that Cooper was used to. But now a new feeling—regret—seemed to overpower everything else. And he couldn't figure out why.

The mag-lev train rocked and swayed down its dark, underground tunnel. But the tunnel was not as dimly lit as Cooper's future. Even at thirty miles a minute, Cooper Hawkes couldn't help but feel he was going nowhere fast.

Where could he go, anyway? There were people bent on killing him in Philadelphia. In fact, he had alienated himself from just about every major North American city. Perhaps, he thought, he could hop a transcontinental and start alienating Europe as well.

The deceleration light came on in the cabin, and the train began to slow in its vacuum tunnel.

"How much ya wanna bet they put us in the frontlines," said a voice across the train.

A dirty man with dirtier hair was eyeing him.

"What are you talking about?" Cooper asked.

The man unbuckled his seat belt and slid into the seat next to him. "I'm talking about us In-Vitros. They'll shove us right in the Aliens' sights to protect themselves," the man said.

The thought made Cooper's hands ball up into fists. Not because it was true. If there was one thing Cooper had learned in the Marines, it was that in the aviator's cavalry, there were no In-Vitros and no flesh-borns. There were only soldiers.

He looked at the dirty man beside him. "How did you know I was an In-Vitro?"

The guy grinned nastily. "You got the look. *Tank eyes.*"

Cooper turned away, but not before catching his own reflection in the dark glass. Tank eyes. Cold as tempered graphite. Empty as the space between galaxies. *No mother, no father, no soul.* The old taunt came back to him. Was it true then? Was his running away proof of some in-born emptiness?

The awful man beside him had Tank eyes too.

"Listen," the man whispered. "Me and a buddy, we got a sweet deal going up in Toronto, smuggling illegal implant chips. We could use a guy like you."

Cooper Hawkes sensed that this would be the most important decision he would ever make in his life. A golden platter was being laid before him. A life in Toronto, better than the life he had known before—or almost certain death in the cold reaches of space.

But the thought of his cavalry comrades kept kicking him in the stomach. And it wasn't just them he'd be deserting. It would be Pags as well.

Shane had once asked him if he had ever lost anyone. The truth was he had never had anyone to lose, until he saw that hole blasted in Pags's chest. He couldn't understand why it hurt so much to think about it, and yet in some strange way that hurt felt good. Because maybe it meant that there was something inside of him after all. Maybe there was a soul.

The mag-lev pulled to a smooth stop inside the Chicago terminal. Cooper grabbed the pathetic man beside him and pushed him up against the wall.

"The answer is no," he growled. "Now get out of my sight before I punch your Tank eyes out the back of your head."

Unaffected, uncaring, this pathetic specimen of a man-made flesh just said, "Suit yourself." He slid out of Cooper's grasp and strolled out the door.

Five minutes later, Cooper hopped on a mag-lev heading east.

Cemeteries held no particular fear for Cooper. The dead were dead. It was a simple fact.

Yet now, as he walked through the desolate hills of Arlington National Cemetery, a horrible, gut-wrenching sensation grew inside him. Each step he took over the neatly trimmed, moonlit grass made him feel worse.

Around him, identical white tombstones rose like blunt teeth, casting moonshadow across three centuries of unvisited graves. Even in that sea of stones, Cooper's sense of direction didn't fail him.

Soon he found himself kneeling over a fresh mound of dirt.

He glanced around as if someone might be watching. It was a foolish thought, since the only people around were six feet under the ground.

Cooper opened his mouth to say something, but it was a long time before any words came out. He wasn't in the habit of speaking to the dead and didn't quite know why he felt compelled to do it now. But he knew he had to. Wanted to.

"Pags," he began. "I wanted to say something when they buried you, but I didn't know what. Anyway, they don't let you say much at those things."

His vision became cloudy. The feeling he had been struggling to contain in his gut forced its way out. Something happened that was completely out of Cooper Hawkes's life experience.

He was crying.

Cooper wiped away a tear and chuckled slightly. "Look at me," he said to the grave. "Did you ever think you'd see me cry?"

He sat down on the mound of dirt. "You were the only guy who was ever okay to me, Pags. I wish somehow you could just . . . sorta . . . know how I feel."

He picked up a handful of earth, squeezing it in his fist. "Maybe right now you can. . . ."

Cooper let the dirt sift through his fingers. "I wish I could know what you feel now," he said to the silent grave. "I thought I knew what it would be like, but seeing you lying there, all bloody . . . I don't know what I'm trying to say. I guess I'm scared, Pags."

It was an admission he'd never made even to himself. He looked up at the stars. They'd always seemed to be so far away. But now the heavens were too close for comfort.

"I wish I could know if anything was worth it."

A flash in the sky caught his attention. Another flash followed, then another—not just in the sky but at the edge of the solar system. That was where the battle was taking place.

The explosions must have been massive to be seen on Earth. But there was no way for Cooper to know whether it was the Earth ships or the Alien ships that were detonating in the sky.

That could be me up there, Cooper thought. The thought was terrible, yet it also gave him a sense of purpose and a strange sort of comfort. Because now, for the first time in his life, he began to feel part of something that was larger than himself.

In the West household dinner went cold and uneaten. It was that way around the world that night, as just about everyone on Earth sat glued to their TV screen, watching mankind's greatest stand against the approaching Alien forces.

With static popping and crackling through the satellite feed, the reporter on the USS *Yorktown*, Earth's largest starcraft carrier, fed news to an anxious world.

"We warn you," said the reporter, "that the images you are about to see are graphic."

Behind him, the blast-buckled corridors of the great ship were lined with bodies. Soot-covered medics struggled to move the wounded out of the corridor.

"The space carriers *Nimitz* and HMS *Montgomery* have been destroyed."

In the living room, the Wests and Shane sat in silence.

The video image changed to that of a space carrier, the *Montgomery*. The ship was shredded so badly it could have been made of paper. It was hard to tell if the spots floating by the wreckage were debris or bodies.

The image changed back to the *Yorktown*, where things seemed to have taken a turn for the worse. Screams and commotion filled the background. The now panicked reporter dodged a falling beam. "There's smoke, electrical flashes—you can hear metal buckling in the bowel of the carrier. . . ."

BLAM! A blast threw the reporter off-screen. The camera fell over on its side, broadcasting a twisted view of the chaos aboard the ship.

There was a flash of static, and then another. Then the picture was gone completely. The screen was filled with nothing but screaming snow.

Nathan jumped up and headed out the door. Shane followed him outside.

In the western quadrant of the sky, the distant flashes faded away. A single fireball erupted and died.

The battle was over. The Earth fleet had been devastated, the 127th defeated.

Before they had time to think about what it all meant, Shane's and Nathan's wrist-coms flashed with an incoming message.

"Attention all aviators of the Marine Corps Aviators' Cavalry. You are ordered to report immediately to base for active duty."

Chapter 13

The 2nd Air Wing, 58th Squadron was ready for battle.

Sparkling new fighters had arrived as fast as they could roll off the assembly lines, stenciled with the names of Lts. Nathan West, Shane Vansen, Cooper Hawkes, and the rest who had trained together in those brutal months when the war had begun.

The Squadron had been back only two days, preparing their planes, practicing maneuvers in the safety of orbital space, when they were given their orders. Soon the barracks would be empty and waiting for the busloads of new recruits, ready to fill the places left by the dead.

They had all watched as the legendary 127th was brought back in—what was left of them. A handful of survivors had been rushed into the base hospital. None of the dead had been brought back, for few bodies are ever recovered from space. Only the living fallen Angels—torn, bandaged, and bloodied—were carried on stretchers into the over-crowded halls of the hospital.

Cooper had arrived just in time to see that. He

was half a day late, but he had returned. No one chewed him out for his tardiness, perhaps because no one expected him to be there at all.

He watched as they carried McQueen in, half his face blown away by the enemy. Then Cooper went to find his comrades and his plane.

The orientation room was packed with hundreds of Marines, all sitting on the edge of their chairs waiting to hear their orders.

"Damphousse heard we're going straight to the line," Shane whispered to Nathan. It was a powerful and heady bit of news, as thrilling as it was terrifying.

"ATTENTION!" shouted Bougus.

In one swift move, the entire orientation room stood to welcome Lieutenant Colonel Fouts into the briefing. Serious and intense, it was Fouts who passed the top-secret orders from the top brass down to the ranks.

"Be seated," said Fouts.

They sat in silence and listened as Fouts relayed their instructions.

"The information you are about to receive is classified Level Red. I don't have to remind you of the consequences of divulging this information." He glanced around the room and singled out Nathan and Shane.

"Fifty-eighth, because of you we caught a major break. Within the wreckage of the Alien recon vehicle recovered during your training mission was an encoded transmission detailing the enemy's battle plan. We have been able to break the code, and now we can anticipate all of the enemy's moves."

He reached down to turn on a projector that put forth a hologram of several parsecs of space. "The enemy intends to attack with extreme intent, two-thirds of its forces at the Groombridge Thirty-four Star System Naval Base in seventy-one hours.

"The Earth forces, the greatest mobilization of military might in history, will surprise and attack from behind the enemy positions." Fouts indicated the two points from which the attack would take place.

"Sir." Shane ventured a question. "How can we possibly get there in seventy-one hours? Even through all the known wormholes, it would take at least a week. Sir."

Fouts nodded. "A new wormhole is projected to open in the Gallileo regions. Another lucky break."

Shane grinned and whispered to Nathan. "It'll work."

Nathan seemed convinced, but it was Cooper, further down the row, who wasn't ready to buy the plan.

"From the captured information," Fouts continued, "we know their planes are faster, with a better rate of climb. But ours are more maneuverable and better armed. In spite of anything you might have heard, we're evenly matched."

The excitement around the room rose.

"Surprise has been their best weapon," Fouts proclaimed. "Now it's ours."

Cooper leaned back in his chair. "It's too easy!" he shouted.

Suddenly all eyes in the room had turned to him. Fouts's gaze became steel.

"Sir," said Cooper. "If the plans weren't planted, then they must know we have them. They'd change their objectives."

Fouts stared him down. "No doubt they felt we would be unable to decipher the transmission. And in fact, it has taken fifty Charno-Quantum computers, interlinked on four continents, to decode the enemy's complex language. Since the decoding, we have found all their movements to be in accord with those captured plans."

Cooper still wasn't buying it, but he kept his mouth shut.

"Sir." Nathan spoke up. "Where are we deploying, sir?"

Fouts hesitated for a moment. "You will be joining forces with the Third Air Wing, who will lead the offensive." On his floating map he pointed to a place far away from the battlefront. "The Fifty-eighth Squadron will be here. Rear left flank."

The Squadron grumbled in protest. "Sir." Nathan didn't even try to hide his frustration. "Why bother telling us the plan if we aren't going to be a part of it?"

"You are a part of it," Fouts insisted angrily. "Rear. Left. Flank."

He paused, then continued firmly. "The Fifty-eighth is to report to the naval space carrier *Saratoga*, across the Jupiter line, by twenty-two forty tomorrow. You'll meet your Squadron commander on board. Dismissed."

The A-43 Hammerheads of the 58th Squadron were lined up in the immense hangar, waiting to fly into battle. Cooper knelt on his wing, with a paintbrush in one hand and a jar of red paint in the other.

Slowly and smoothly, he began to paint on the steel hull just behind the cockpit. For hundreds of years, it had been a tradition to name the plane you took into battle. Cooper knew what his ship's name would be. Whatever misgivings he had about the mission, he knew he would fly into war. He'd known it from the moment he'd left Pags's grave and headed back to the Marine base. Seeing his plane, stenciled with the words LIEUTENANT COOPER HAWKES, confirmed it. He knew this was a responsibility he couldn't run from.

Lieutenant Cooper Hawkes.

He let the words play over in his mind again and again. A title like that wasn't given randomly. It was something you earned. It amazed Cooper that he could earn such a thing.

Nathan and Shane stormed into the hangar.

"I should request to be transferred to the Third Air Wing," Nathan fumed.

"I'll back you if you do," Shane said. "I'll request transfer too."

Cooper shook his head. "Come on, Lieutenants," he said, enjoying the way the word rolled off his tongue. "They gave us our orders. It's our job to follow them."

"Is that so?" Nathan asked. "Don't you think we have a right to follow through with what we started, Hawkes? We were the ones who brought back that Alien. It's because of us that they even *have* that break. We should be the ones leading this battle, not watching from the back row."

Cooper shrugged. "I thought we were part of a team," he said. "Somebody has to take rear left flank. If it's us, it's us."

"Afraid to be in the frontlines, Hawkes?" challenged Nathan.

But Cooper didn't feel like a challenge. Not today. "No more than you," he said. He turned to Shane. "Vansen, you remember on Mars, when we came to that Alien ship? You put me in the 'back row,' remember?"

Shane nodded.

"Well, if I had done what I was supposed to do, instead of complaining about it, I might have seen the Alien before he shot Pags."

Shane shook her head. "It was too dark. And besides, if it hadn't been for you, that Alien might have gotten away."

Cooper shrugged. "My point is, if they need us to pull up the rear, then let's not blow it by complaining."

The point got through to Nathan. He grinned. "Hawkes, correct me if I'm wrong . . . but I think they turned you into a soldier."

Cooper looked down at his hand. Some of the paint had spilled across his palm. He touched a fingertip to it and drew small red lines on both cheeks. "I prefer to think of myself as a warrior," he said with a smirk. Then he took his red-painted hand and placed it firmly against the hull of his ship. The fiery hand print left behind was the finishing touch to the name he had given it: "Pags's Payback."

Three hours later, the 58th Squadron of the 2nd Air Wing rolled out of their hangars. Nathan's fighter, "Beyond and Back," followed by "Pags's Payback," and Shane's fighter with Damphousse, Wang, and the rest bringing up the rear, thundered out onto the tarmac.

On the ground beneath them, Bougus saluted as each plane wheeled past.

They took off in twenty-second intervals. Before long they blasted through the ionosphere, escaped Earth's gravity, and flew in formation toward the Jupiter line to rendezvous with the *Saratoga*.

Chapter 14

At full burn, it took just over thirty-six hours to reach the *Saratoga*. The 58th Squadron flew in perfect formation led by Shane, whose Hammerhead was at the point of the wedge of ships flying toward Jupiter and the great spacecraft carrier in the planet's orbit.

With the massive planet looming before them, Shane increased the magnification on her Heads Up Display. There on the HUD screen was the grainy image of the *Saratoga*. Incredibly huge as the ship was, it appeared as little more than a speck on the HUD.

She turned on her radio. "Gold Leader, confirm *Saratoga* position at thirty-two point five mega-statute miles."

She waited for Nathan to respond but heard nothing. With Shane's on-board computer controlling the formation, all the pilots had taken scheduled sleep shifts. But no one should have been asleep now, not when they were this close to the *Saratoga*. She called out to Nathan again.

"Come in, Gold Leader. Confirm."

Nathan, leading the formation's right wing, was preoccupied with his LIDAR—his Light Detection and Ranging Device. For the last minute or so, his HUD screen showed nothing but static. He knew these fighters had rolled quickly off the production line, and he began to wonder if perhaps his LIDAR had some bugs that would get him killed in battle. If it was malfunctioning, he had better find out now.

"Just a second," he answered Shane. "I'm getting interference on the LIDAR."

He flipped some switches, increasing energy to the LIDAR array, and ran the image through a series of filters. It was soon perfectly clear why his HUD screen had filled with static. His screen wasn't malfunctioning. It was being jammed.

Out of nowhere, a triple-winged ship spun across the screen, trying to fly past the formation without being noticed.

"Red Leader! Confirm bandit! A recon vehicle on the LIDAR!"

To Nathan's surprise, Red Leader responded almost immediately. It was the most attentive Nathan had ever seen Cooper Hawkes.

"Confirm! Confirm!" Cooper shouted. "LIDAR channel four, bogie: ten o'clock!"

If nothing else, their training had taught them quick response. And, as always, Shane made a rapid and right decision.

"Alter intercept angle thirty degrees!" she ordered. "Blue team, White team, watch six! Hack!"

Instantly, the wedge of the Squadron broke up, giving each team a wider perspective and a better shot at the enemy.

The standard maneuver sent adrenaline coursing through Nathan's veins. This was not a simulation. Sergeant Major Bougus wasn't standing by ready to pop the cockpit and chew them out if something went wrong.

Soon they were on the Alien's tail. Nathan could see the Alien spacecraft now through his canopy. It was the same type of ship they had found on Mars: so black, it almost disappeared against the deadness of space. It spat out a dull purple exhaust from a fuel no scientist on Earth had been able to synthesize.

"Twelve o'clock high," Nathan announced. He powered up his remaining weapons and locked in the retinal targeting system.

"Confirm," Shane said. "Let's light the pipes and head downtown."

Shane was above him and Cooper below. All three of them simultaneously pulled back on their throttles. Nathan felt the thrust push him deep into his seat.

By now two wings from the 58th had come in around the enemy, trying to block its escape. But the Alien ship's speed was so great that it shot through the hole before the formation could close.

Then the Alien craft made a sudden, unexpected turn before any of them could lock their weapons on it.

"He jinked!" said Shane. "Scram! Scram!"

Nathan saw her fire. She missed the Alien ship. And then it was gone.

Nathan looked in his HUD display but saw nothing but static again.

"Lost it," Cooper said.

Nathan played with the switches on his LIDAR, but it was no use. "It went below us like a fish on a line," he said. He imagined the Alien ship hiding somewhere beneath them, waiting for a chance to circle back and open fire, blasting through the entire formation.

"Let's go fishing," Cooper suggested. But Shane didn't go for it.

"Negative," she said. "Don't have the fuel. Return to designated course. I'll call Space Com and report ACM with the enemy."

Nathan sighed. Their first real taste of aerial combat, and it was over too fast for them to even know what happened. And even so, it was more terrifying than he imagined it would be. He hadn't felt the terror until now that it was over. He wondered if it was always that way in battle, the fear not setting in until the exchange was played out.

Before them Jupiter loomed closer. It was still millions of miles away, but it filled up half the view.

The Squadron regrouped and continued to the *Saratoga*.

If a naval aircraft carrier was impressive, the super-starcraft carrier *Saratoga* was awe-inspiring—something you couldn't imagine until you actually saw it.

Without gravity to limit its shape, it had several flight decks built off its upper and lower hull as well as its sides.

Its armored bridge was flanked with heavy artillery, and it was filled with nearly one hundred docking bays to receive incoming fighters.

The Squadron maneuvered itself toward the docking bays. Once across the portal threshold, each ship was sucked deep into the great carrier by a smooth magnetic pulse.

Then, with a grinding of metal clamps and releases, the cockpits themselves were detached from the fighters and elevated to the upper flight deck.

The moment the upper flight deck was pressurized, dozens of support personnel flooded the deck to service the cockpits as the canopies opened and the pilots emerged.

It was Cooper who noticed that the service crew was moving incredibly quickly.

"Is it just me, or do they seem a little panicked?" Cooper asked Nathan as he got out.

The crews were already running diagnostics on the cockpits and downloading new software to prevent further LIDAR jamming. Cooper and Nathan turned to see Shane practically forced away from her cockpit. The crews were behaving as if a single second lost would mean the difference between life and death for the service personnel.

Wang came up behind them. "Maybe it's always this way aboard a carrier."

Nathan shook his head. "I don't think so."

"Whatever it is," Cooper said, "I think we're about to find out."

A shout of "Attention!" rang out on the deck.

The pilots all snapped to obey as Captain Eichner strode across the flight deck toward them. The service crew seemed to be exempt from the order; they continued frantically preparing the ships for battle.

Eichner wasted no time in idle conversation.

"Squadron Fifty-eight, report to the briefing area immediately!"

Shane took a step forward. "Sir, what's going on?"

"Space Com checked out your report of the enemy recon vehicle," he told her. "Our radio telescopes have since found . . . not only no trace of enemy troops in the Groombridge system, but a force massing near the orbit of Saturn. Our own backyard."

Cooper gritted his teeth. The enemy plans had been a setup after all. He knew he should have trusted his instincts. He should have raised his voice and *made* his superiors listen.

Shane clasped his shoulder, as if to say, You were right, but we can only move forward now.

"At this point," said Eichner, "we don't need their plans to know in which direction they're headed."

Nathan, Cooper, and Shane looked at each other. The same thought occurred to the three of them.

With practically all the Earth's forces amassed light-years away at Groombridge, they were the only ones left to stop the massive Alien force headed toward Earth.

A single Squadron of green, untried pilots.

The 58th wasn't destined to be a minor part of the stand for humanity. They were to be humanity's only stand.

Chapter 15

Desperate times bring out the best and the worst in people. For Cooper Hawkes, it had always brought out the worst. Yet here, at the forefront of humanity's darkest hour, Cooper found himself rising above and beyond anything he had ever dreamed he could be. His past failures were forgotten. The fact that he was a Tank held no meaning anymore, not in the face of the Alien menace.

Now the rest of the Squadron looked up to him. Him, Nathan, and Shane. And he knew that it would be the actions of the three of them that would determine either the salvation or destruction of humanity.

Shane, too, wrestled with the weight of this responsibility as they strode, in double time, to the briefing room. She wondered if her parents were out there, somewhere, watching. Were they proud of her or turning away in sorrow, unable to watch their daughter lead a group of hopelessly inexperienced pilots to their doom? She had never been religious, but now she prayed for the strength to do what she needed to do. If they succeeded they would be the greatest of heroes. She wondered if that was what the 127th had thought before being blown out of the sky.

The only picture that occupied Nathan's thoughts was a finely focused one. For him, all of humanity came down to a few faces: his family's, and Kylen's. He could not bear to imagine his father's vision coming true; Alien ships cresting the distant mountains, laying waste to everything in their path. He couldn't bear to imagine his younger brothers being blown to bits by carelessly lethal Alien blasters. Whether Kylen was dead or alive, he knew he didn't want to live to see anyone else he loved destroyed by these terrible beings. He would rather die trying to stop them. Still there was no peace in knowing that.

The briefing room on board the *Saratoga* was a glassed-in, high-tech enclosure beside the battle bridge. A collection of projectors and state-of-the-art holographic display screens were set before the rows of seats now occupied by the 58th Squadron. In the center, a single table was filled with more equipment and notes.

Captain Eichner stepped into the doorway as the 58th stood at attention. He eyed them solemnly, clearly concerned that the war was going to hinge on less than two dozen pilots fresh out of Loxley.

Behind him, they saw a familiar face. Or half of one.

McQueen stepped to the front of the room. The

scars from the 127th's defeat ravaged his face—deep crevices burned beyond medical science's ability to repair. But apparently the wound was only skin deep. They could all sense that his fighting spirit was very much intact. He was, in fact, the only one of the surviving Angels still on active duty.

He looked them over and said simply, "Sit down."

Eichner left them to their business. The second he was gone, McQueen grabbed the table laden with notes and equipment.

SLAM! He flipped it to the other side of the room, sending every device shattering on the floor, papers flying.

As the debris settled, McQueen pulled up a chair and sat down in front of them.

"I want to be able to look into your eyes," he said to the startled group. He did exactly that as he spoke; he singled out each and every one of them.

"Courage," he began. "Honor. Dedication. Sacrifice." He paused to make sure they were all following him. They were.

"Those," McQueen continued, "were the words they used to get you here. But now the only word that means anything to you is 'life.' *Your* life. The lives of your buddies."

It hit home better than any other words the military had given them. It cut through all the pretenses. It cut through all ranks.

"In an hour, maybe two," he continued, "you'll

either be alive or you'll be dead. And for the next hour, this is your best chance of staying alive."

He went on to tell them what they had to do. They needed no fancy visuals from McQueen, only his words—blunt and to the point.

"The Trojan asteroid belt trails Jupiter's orbit. Your objective is to hide in this debris, which may be as difficult as engaging the enemy. You'll have to react to the pitch and yaw of the asteroids to keep out of sight and shielded from their LIDAR. Intelligence says they should fly right past you. Then you'll jump 'em."

The Squadron began to shift in their seats, lean forward. Maybe there was a glimmer of hope—for them, for the war.

"No one's asking you to wax their tails," McQueen advised. "Your goal is to *stall* them. Our forces at Groombridge have doubled back, and with any luck will soon be passing through the Kali wormhole. If you can successfully delay the enemy, you'll have reinforcements appearing from behind them and from out of the sun. And that's when we teach them about payback."

As intense as the look on McQueen's face was, it suddenly became darker, angrier. "Listen closely to what I'm about to tell you. I'm here because I've already been in a knife fight with them. They come at you in groups, and they have a low angle of attack, so keep your noses level. That could be tough; the planes you've been issued have an upgripe in the retro-thrusters.

"And one more thing," he added. His eyes fell on Cooper. "It's okay to be scared. See you in an hour."

When he was gone, Damphousse shook her head. "An hour." She turned to the others. "I guess it's true what they say about time dilation. This is going to be the longest hour I've ever spent."

The 58th Squadron returned to the upper flight deck to find the chaos they'd left behind intensified as technicians made last-minute checks of the equipment.

As Nathan approached his cockpit, he could only imagine how many more technicians were racing around down below, preparing the bodies of the fighters for battle.

In the hour they'd had after the briefing, there had been very little talk. Nathan had kept his silence, as if uttering a word might break his concentration.

He watched Wang, Damphousse, and several others pass what might be their last minutes together. He watched Shane, too, as she pushed out words of encouragement to the more anxious pilots.

Now the waiting time had gone.

As he prepared to step into his cockpit, he turned to see Cooper checking his flightsuit.

Cooper's face no longer had the contemptuously cold look it had when he'd first arrived at Loxley. His face was directed, focused. Just like Nathan's.

For the longest time Nathan had hated the Tank with a passion that had little to do with Cooper Hawkes the man. But there was no room for that now.

"Hawkes," he shouted.

Cooper looked up.

Nathan wanted to say he was sorry, wanted to let Cooper know that he was an equal, part of the team now. But Nathan couldn't put it into words. So Hawkes did it for him.

"Yeah, I know," said Hawkes with the slightest grin.

Nathan smiled in spite of the frantic tension all around them and stepped into his cockpit. Like a precision racetrack pit crew, the technicians strapped him in and sealed the canopy.

The lesson that Bougus had given them after their first disastrous simulation wasn't lost on Nathan or any of the fliers who had been there. Although they flew separate planes, they were connected by an invisible tether that made them what they were—a team.

The alarm sounded. The support crews cleared the deck and the airlock door came down behind them. A sudden, intense wind rose and fell as the deck depressurized to the vacuum of space.

Nathan caught sight of Shane in her cockpit, facing him. She gave him a thumbs-up, and he returned it, just as the cockpits were lowered through the floor and locked onto the bodies of the Hammerheads that were already positioned for launch on the lower flight deck.

Nathan felt his hair stand on end as the mass-accelerator engaged. The force propelled his entire ship through the length of the carrier and slingshot him into the star-filled void.

Their thrusters were at full burn. The *Saratoga* disappeared behind the 58th Squadron in a matter of seconds. They headed around to the dark side of Jupiter and to the deadly asteroid field that lay beyond.

Chapter 16

Shane had hated the asteroid simulations back in basic training. She had come through them all with flying colors, but it didn't mean she had enjoyed them.

She had simply learned to judge and anticipate the movements of the sim-asteroids as she had maneuvered between them. But sim-asteroids were all roughly the same shape, and they came in only three sizes.

Here, there was no telling what they would come across. They had no idea how the asteroids would be shaped, how densely they'd be packed, or how their gravity might affect the Hammerheads' flight patterns.

As the 58th approached, the asteroid belt looked like specks of dust trailing the red-eyed planet. But as the Squadron drew closer, the specks grew to boulders. The boulders grew into mountain-sized chunks of stone, drifting randomly past one another.

It was an obstacle course no pilot should ever be asked to run.

"Stay tight," Shane instructed. "Thrusters at ten percent. Let's go for cover."

They broke formation and maneuvered into the shadows of the asteroids coming at them from all sides.

Total concentration was needed now, thought Shane. Being able to see out the back of her head would have helped, too, but without that, she and the rest would have to rely on instinct and full attention to their instruments and thruster stick.

As Shane looked at the field around her, something caught her eye. A Hammerhead, trying to evade an asteroid to its starboard, hadn't seen the one looming up from below.

"Red-four, you're too close," she radioed. "Coming up at nine o'clock."

Red-four responded with a single thruster. Too late.

The asteroid clipped his wing and sent him spinning into the larger one.

"Red-four!" Shane called. But the only response was a fiery blast as Red-four smashed against the asteroid.

Shane had to turn her eyes away. *Who was Red-four?* She knew every name and assignment in the Squadron, but right now she couldn't remember who it had been. All she could think about was how horrible it was for the pilot to die without his wing commander even remembering his name.

When she looked up again, she realized that the explosion of Red-four had changed the trajectory of all the asteroids in her immediate vicinity. The same one that had done in Red-four was now spinning right toward her.

She jinked right, sending her craft into a roll that corkscrewed her around the asteroid. She pulled her stick to the left, taking her ship around another chunk of stone before she finally leveled off. For the moment she was out of harm's way.

Further off, another flash of light signaled a second lost fighter.

Wang reported the loss. It had been Gold-three. His name was Osborne. Shane promised herself she would remember that.

The "Beyond and Back" perfectly mimicked the motion of the asteroid above it. It hovered just a few delicate meters away from the crushing rock. Inside the ship, Nathan studied his instruments, making sure the readings were all correct. He'd been given the responsibility of communicating with the *Saratoga*.

He turned his radio on a coded band the enemy couldn't pick up. "*Saratoga*, this is Blue Leader. We're tied on."

There was a pause. No response. And then, after a few more seconds: "Copy that, Blue Leader. Will advise."

Something didn't sound right. Keeping one hand

on the stick to negotiate the asteroids, Nathan engaged his LIDAR. Instantly his Heads Up Display switched from asteroid vectors to a wide view of local space.

There was the enemy.

Just a microparsec away, thousands of tiny green dots danced on Nathan's screen, too many to count. The smaller crafts were surrounding a core of motherships. Altogether, the force was probably enough to lay waste to Earth in a matter of moments.

Nathan watched the screen. From what he could see, they were changing course—*away* from the asteroid field. Could the enemy know they were there?

No, thought Nathan. If there was one thing he knew about the enemy, it was that they always took the offensive. If they had been spotted they would have been attacked, plain and simple. It was more likely that the huge Alien attack force was just being careful, giving the asteroid field a wide berth so they didn't risk losing any ships.

This was supposed to be an ambush. But an ambush worked only if the enemy came your way.

"*Saratoga,*" hailed Nathan. "LIDAR shows the enemy to be—"

But the *Saratoga* cut him off before he could finish. "Affirmative, Blue Leader. Will advise," the voice said more strongly.

It was a different voice this time. A stronger voice. McQueen's.

Nathan couldn't believe they were just sitting there, letting them pass.

"Hold your position," McQueen ordered.

Hold your position. Wait them out. Those were the orders. Nathan was bound to obey them. But he hoped beyond hope that something would bring the enemy their way.

Cooper Hawkes had a tendency to pocket things of interest from time to time, a habit born from years of having to live on the street. Little good had ever come of it—until now.

As the Alien force moved further and further away, Cooper pulled out the gold micro-CD he had taken from the Mars tracking station.

He had jury-rigged a disk drive in his cockpit for his own amusement. Now he slipped the disk in. Rock music began to blare out from his cockpit. Pink Floyd, to be exact. It carried over the coded frequency radio to each Hammerhead and back to the *Saratoga*.

"What the heck . . . ?" he heard Shane say.

Cooper let the pounding music fill him. Over the past few months, he had learned to be a team player, but he was still best at being a renegade. And now a renegade was exactly what this mission needed.

He eased his stick forward, thrusting clear of the asteroid field. Then he cranked his engine to full power and headed straight for the enemy.

This one was for Pags.

He could hear in his radio the commotion his move had caused. They all knew what he was up to. He was going to bait the enemy past them. He smiled as he remembered how that single enemy craft had gone beneath them like a fish on a line. Well, it was time to see if this school of fish would go after the bait.

Over his radio he heard Nathan say, "I'm going to help him out."

"Negative, Blue Leader," he heard Shane respond. "He'll bring 'em past. Wait 'til we can all go."

Cooper was coming up on the enemy faster than he thought. The sky seemed packed solid with their ships.

"I'm goin' in, fangs out," Cooper radioed back. Then he tore into the tail of the enemy, firing at will.

The enemy's pack was so dense, he destroyed a ship with practically every blast. He was literally tunneling through the enemy, clearing a path for himself, obliterating everything in his way.

He jinked hard to the right to avoid smashing against one of the massive, pylonlike motherships. Racing forward at twice their speed, he took aim at the lead formation. Perfect! He blew the six forward-most Alien fighters to oblivion.

But now they were firing on him. He had no choice but to take a wild, careening arc around the enemy's left flank. He cut through space as fast as his engines could carry him, back toward the safety of the asteroid field.

Behind him, the enemy ships quickly changed formation, going on attack.

"They're snagged!" Cooper announced gleefully. "I'm reeling 'em in."

He threw his ship into a roll, but not quite fast enough. Enemy fire blasted past him, narrowly missing his wings. Just a few seconds more . . .

The asteroid field came crashing toward him, engulfing his ship like the mother of all hailstorms. In an instant, boulders twice the size of his vessel were blurring past all around him. It took all of his focus to keep from hitting the mammoth rocks head on.

Behind him, the enemy continued to fire. Four enemy fighters had already entered the asteroid field. One was instantly taken out by an asteroid that had eclipsed its path, but the other three "fish" were right on Cooper's tail.

BLAM! An enemy blast detonated a small asteroid right in front of him. The debris scattered—some of it was sent swirling off into space, but the rest pummeled his canopy. He tried to roll right, to evade the enemy. Tried . . . but his stick wouldn't move.

"My controls froze!" he shouted out. His HUD showed that the enemy had locked on to him. In front of him an asteroid loomed in the center of his path.

This was it. He knew he was dead.

Then, over the radio, he heard McQueen.

"Kill your left thrusters, you stupid Tank!"

Cooper hit the thruster with one hand, yanked hard on the controls with the other.

His ship turned, barely rolling past the asteroid. It was so close he could practically feel the huge boulder scraping his belly. The enemy ship was not as lucky. Still locked in position, Cooper saw it disappear in a burst of flame and dust as it hit the asteroid.

Cooper took a deep breath. When he looked up again, he wasn't alone.

The 58th Squadron had come out of their hiding positions and had begun to engage the enemy.

Chapter 17

Damphousse got the first kill. She forced her fire down the enemy's throat and blew one ship to pieces as she rocketed through it.

Wang locked on to another. His fire clipped its wing and sent it careening out of control into an asteroid.

Shane held her fire and took stock of the situation around her. More enemy fighters were headed into the asteroid field, always in clusters of four, always in the same formation.

"McQueen was right, they fly in gangs," she reminded the others. Focusing on the pattern rather than on the individual fighters, she blew one whole gang out of the sky.

"*Hoo-yah!* Let's go downtown!" she shouted.

The 58th Squadron hit their thrusters. Pulling out of the asteroid field, they headed straight into the heart of the enemy.

Nathan emerged from the asteroid field with a gang of four on his tail. He managed to blow two of them away with his rear guns, but the other two were still firing on him.

Around him, in all directions, explosions lit up the dark sky. They weren't just Alien ships. They were Hammerheads as well.

Blue-four.

Gold-two.

But they couldn't stop to count the casualties now.

Over his radio, he heard, "This is Red Leader. I need a little help." Cooper never asked for help. . . .

He found Cooper on his LIDAR, still deep in the asteroid field, still trying to shake the Aliens on his tail.

"I'm on it," Nathan said as he did a barrel roll and plunged back into the asteroid field.

In a moment, he could see Pags's Payback, jinking wildly between enemy fire and the asteroids in its path.

BAM! Nathan fired and sent one of the Alien fighters careening into a nearby asteroid. But the one remaining fighter had already locked on to Cooper. Nathan could do nothing but watch as it fired.

Cooper took the blast in the tail. His right engine sputtered, then stopped altogether.

"I'm losing thrust!" he yelled.

The enemy veered around an asteroid and locked on again, coming in for the kill.

There was only one thing Nathan could do. It

would be a tricky maneuver, but it was the only way to save Hawkes.

Behind him, two Aliens were still breathing down his neck. In front of him the crippled "Pags's Payback" and the Alien fighter disappeared behind a giant asteroid.

Nathan pulled on his controls with all of his strength and forced his Hammerhead into an inverted loop around the asteroid. He would loop around the asteroid in a tight bank and come at Cooper head on. Neither Cooper nor the enemy would see him until he was flying down their throats. He hoped his judgment had been right and that Cooper would react quickly enough.

The asteroid spun past him as he made the loop. Suddenly, Cooper was in his sights, heading straight toward him.

"Hit the deck!" Nathan shouted.

Cooper flashed past him, missing a head-on by a fraction of an inch. Nathan could have sworn he'd seen Cooper in his cockpit, his eyes squeezed tightly shut.

As soon as Cooper was past, Nathan pulled out of the roll. Behind him, the ships following him continued on their course. They smashed into the ship that had been following Cooper, exploding in a hot blast of purple and green fuel. A white-hot fireball was all that was left of them.

Victory screams exploded over the radio.

"Not so fast," Nathan heard Cooper say. "There's a bandit locked on Shane."

Nathan located Shane on his LIDAR. She was out of his range. A single bogie was close on her tail, and although she was trying every evasive maneuver in the book, the Alien fighter stayed locked on.

Cooper was closest and was already heading toward her. But with his crippled thruster he'd never make it. Nathan went full throttle, hoping there were no asteroids in his way.

Shane was all alone, and she knew it.

Damphousse, Wang, and the rest of the Squadron were out engaging one of the motherships. Only Nathan and Cooper were anywhere nearby. Although Nathan was coming up fast, Shane knew he wasn't going to be fast enough.

She jinked to the right, but not in time. A blast breathed across her right side, singeing the wing black.

She went into a full roll in a last-ditch attempt to free herself, but the enemy rolled with her and fired again. She cringed, feeling the blast hit her somewhere behind. She had no idea how bad the damage was.

BOOM! BOOM!

For an instant, Shane thought she had been hit again. Then she realized the shots had come from high above her. The explosion lighting up the aster-oids around her was actually the Alien spacecraft—disintegrating into bits.

There were no words for the relief she felt or for her gratitude for her teammate.

"Hoo-yah! Popped him good, Nathan!"

There was a pause on the other end.

"But I didn't fire," Nathan said.

"It wasn't me either," said Cooper.

"But . . . who got the kill?" Shane turned her eyes in the direction of the blasts to see—

Starcraft carriers!

Not just a few, but dozens. With hundreds of Hammerheads. They were coming up from behind them and out of the sun.

The Groombridge forces had made it through the wormhole!

Hammerheads charged the enemy fighters, and the carriers fired off their heavy guns, devastating the Alien motherships.

Suddenly the highly organized enemy seemed to be moving at random. The Alien motherships changed course one way, and then another, as the Earth forces came in from two different angles.

Shane, Nathan, and Cooper watched in awe as every remaining enemy ship headed up and out, in full retreat.

The Earth forces continued to fire on the retreating

enemy. By the time they were out of range, at least three Alien motherships had been destroyed, along with countless fighters.

Shane, Nathan, and West sat speechless in their cockpits as the rest of the 58th flew back and joined them.

"So, is that what they call 'mission accomplished'?" they heard Damphousse ask ecstatically.

"Looks like we just bought ourselves one more hour," Wang responded.

It was only as they headed back to base that they began to realize just what it was that they had done.

Chapter 18

On the pristine Marine Academy grounds, President Chartwell addressed the aviators of the "Battle of the Belt," as the media was already calling it.

Cooper Hawkes stood in the front row beside Shane, Nathan, and the other surviving members of the 58th Squadron. The medal that hung around his neck was heavier than he thought it would be. Its golden spikes reflected the afternoon sun, giving it a spectacular glow.

It was still strange for Cooper to think that someone, *anyone*, would present him with a medal like this. He had never been given anything. But stranger still was the thought that this medal that hung around his neck was something he had earned. Something he deserved.

Chartwell's speech was long-winded, but as far as the 58th was concerned, it could have gone on forever. Rarely could the President of the United Nations be bothered to speak at a military ceremony—but the 58th had already become legend.

"Because of the valiant efforts of the Marine

Corps 58th Squadron," proclaimed Chartwell, "the many peoples of Earth breathe a single sigh of relief. So today we honor them."

Applause rose from the huge audience in attendance.

Shane's sisters were there. So were Nathan's parents and brothers. And as for Cooper, well, the medal would have to be enough.

Chartwell continued, "I believe even that great twentieth-century leader Winston Churchill would agree when I say that never in the field of conflict has so much been owed by so many to so few."

The applause rang out again, but the 58th remained at fine military attention. Not even the glimmer of a smile could be seen on their faces.

"We of Earth are proud and grateful," said Chartwell. "Celebrate well . . . although we know this break in the storm is momentary. The thunder shall return, the lightning will certainly strike again."

It was a truth they were all painfully aware of. They had won this battle, but the enemy had not been destroyed. It would be only a matter of time before they regrouped and launched another offensive.

This war was far from over.

Nathan West, Shane Vansen, and Cooper Hawkes had attempted the impossible, and succeeded. Thrown together by fate, the three of them had joined their strengths to save the world. They ignited the 58th into a fighting machine against humanity's darkest enemy, turning a losing battle into victory.

That evening, after receiving their medals, they gathered in the towering reception hall of the academy. Champagne flowed freely, and the 58th happily endured the heartfelt congratulations of everyone present, from the stoic handshake of Sergeant Major Bougus to the tearful embraces of Nathan's mother.

Shane Vansen, both stunning and commanding in her full-dress uniform, took the last two glasses of champagne from a passing waiter and brought one to Cooper. She had noticed how, through most of the reception, Cooper stood against one pillar or another clearly feeling out of place. Shane could tell he simply didn't know how to be social. All those years of loathing and prejudice the world had hurled at him had left their mark. It was no wonder he felt alone even when surrounded by so many kind people.

Shane handed him one of the glasses and kept the other for herself.

"You can step in and talk to people," she said with a smile. "They're not going to bite."

Cooper shrugged. "I guess it's not my kind of party."

"Come on over," she said gently. "We're going to have a toast."

Cooper nodded and moved with her through the crowd, toward Nathan, Wang, and Damphousse.

Shane raised her glass, but before she could

speak, she noticed McQueen making his way to them. They all straightened to attention—not because they had to, but out of sheer respect.

"Congratulations," said McQueen.

Shane was glad he had approached them. She had been wanting to say something to him about his encouragement that day on the *Saratoga*. He had cut through all of the rhetoric and had reminded them of the point of it all: simple survival.

"Sir," she began, "your advice, your words that day, they kept us alive—"

But McQueen cut her off. "Save it," he said. "You'll have all the time in the world to thank me. I've just been assigned as your Squadron commander."

It was something they were all pleased to hear. But as was his style, McQueen cut their excitement short. "And if you ever pull anything like what you pulled in that asteroid belt while you're under my command," he said sternly, "the only metal you'll be wearing are cuffs in the brig."

McQueen walked away, leaving them all to ponder his words.

Shane felt her spirits cave in a little. But she understood why he had said that. After all, McQueen was part of the old 127th, and he knew how dangerous a cocky attitude could be. The scars on his face would be a constant reminder of that. The last thing he wanted was to lead a Squadron full of big shots and hotheads.

McQueen's curt words made Shane realize, despite all this temporary glory, that someday, perhaps very soon, they would be out there again, flying in and out of the enemy's sights. No amount of glory would help them then. All they would have would be each other to keep themselves alive.

It was Damphousse who remembered the toast. She raised her glass, and the others followed.

"To Pags," she said.

"To Pags," echoed Shane. "And to being alive for one more hour."

Cooper Hawkes clinked his glass against Shane's, Nathan's, and each of the others'. In a few moments, the others had drifted into the crowd, pulled away by people anxious to talk to the heroes of the day. Cooper was left to himself again, alone in the crowd.

All evening Cooper had felt uneasy. It wasn't just the stuffy party—it went far deeper than that. He'd spent most of his life seeing the world as something he could use, something to benefit himself. Now, to his amazement, he'd found his place in the world—and it was with a team of pilots dedicated to saving others.

But he wasn't being entirely selfless, was he? There was something addictive about the excitement. Even now he longed for the rush of fear and exhilaration of battle. He had blown countless Alien ships out of the sky. He'd tasted victory once. He was ready for more.

It brought back to mind something he had told

Nathan and Shane. He had said it to be clever, but now it struck home as something that was also true. *He was a warrior.* From this moment on, he would live a warrior's life. Someday he'd die a warrior's death. He hoped that day would be a long, long way off. There would be many more battles to fight, many more victories to celebrate first.

It was then that Pags's mother found him. She and her husband had made the rounds, congratulating all the others of the 58th. Cooper had disappeared into the woodwork earlier, not wanting to talk to them, not knowing how. Now he was cornered.

"You know, Lieutenant Hawkes," she began, "my son wrote about you in his letters."

"Is that so." Cooper shifted uncomfortably. "Well, I've changed since then. . . ."

"He said you have a good soul."

Cooper swallowed hard, trying not to let one of his new, unfamiliar emotions out at this particular time. How could he tell this woman that her son might still be alive, if one stupid Tank had been watching like he'd been supposed to?

"Listen ma'am," he began. "About your son—"

" 'Pags's Payback,' " she said, cutting him off.

It caught Cooper off guard. She knew about that? He stammered, not knowing what to say.

"For the longest time," she continued thoughtfully, "I couldn't stop thinking that Michael's death was senseless, that it served no purpose. But now, I think about you and your friends. . . . Maybe Michael died so there would *be* a 'Pags's Payback.' Maybe he died so that you would do what you did to turn the war. Thanks to you, I know he died for a reason."

Cooper just stood there, unable to say a word.

"I hope you'll visit us on your next leave," she said.

Cooper managed to mumble his thanks for the invitation, and she left.

He doubted he'd ever take her up on it.

But then again, maybe he would.

Long before the reception began to wind down, Nathan West stepped out of the great hall and into the silence of a cool night. The academy grounds were shrouded in the darkness of the new moon.

Nathan had shaken so many hands he could feel a cramp in his fingers. He had smiled so many polite smiles his cheeks had begun to hurt. And yet, through it all, he couldn't help feeling like an impostor.

He didn't feel like a hero. Despite what everyone said and what had happened out there in the asteroid belt.

Far behind him, he could hear the sounds of the reception. In front of him, a long reflecting pool shimmered in the gentle breeze.

Kylen . . .

No matter what he achieved, there would always be Kylen. He could not believe that she was dead.

Somehow, no matter how far away, he knew he would have sensed it if she had died. Some part of him was convinced that somewhere, in the endless reaches of space, she was still alive.

He thought of the letter he had written her that last day, before he had naively stowed away aboard the Tellus transport. The letter spoke of how, in so many million years, long after life had vanished from Earth, the sun would swell and then collapse in upon itself. How so many other systems, larger, older, would continue to breathe even as our solar system died.

If that's how long it takes, he had written, *all right. If I must wait that long, then I will. Because when I think of this, nothing is more desirable than the hope of watching that last day, when the sun flickers out, with you beside me.*

He knew, now more than ever, that he could never stop loving her.

Nathan gripped the medal resting upon his chest and tore it from his neck. With all the strength he could muster, he hurled it at the stars.

There could be no medals. There could be no glory. He would not be a hero.

Not until he had found Kylen, as he swore he would.

He watched as the medal spun end over end into the sky above him, seeming to disappear against the deep field of stars, swallowed by the vastness of space.